CHRISTMAS SILKS

PATRICIA D. EDDY

Editing by Jayne Frost

Cover Design by Melody Barber

JUST FOR YOU

Join my Unstoppable Readers' Group for sneak peeks, behind the scenes updates from my writing cave, and more. http://patriciadeddy.com.

A favor...

After you finish this book, you'd make my day if you'd take a few moments to leave a review and tell your friends about Christmas Silks. You can leave a review where you purchased the book and on Goodreads.

1

*N*ick Fairhaven brushed the felt.

Hit me.

The dealer flipped the Jack of Spades onto Nick's cards.

"Bust at twenty-four," the dealer announced.

Nick sighed. Not his night. Again. He stared down at the chips scattered in front of him. Less than a thousand left. With a flip of a hundred-dollar chip to the dealer, Nick pushed away from the table. He shouldn't have come down to Atlantic City today. But with Candy gone, his house felt empty. If his brother hadn't been recuperating from a gunshot wound and unable to get out of bed, Nick would have gone to visit Alex and his girlfriend. But Alex made a terrible patient, and dealing with the man's poor attitude *and* watching the brother he'd idolized for the past dozen years too infirm to stand without assistance wasn't his idea of a good time.

Sliding the last seven-fifty across the cage to the cashier, he glanced up at the board. "Put it all on the Colts, love."

As Nick reclined in one of the posh chairs in front of a

wall of TVs, he wondered just how much worse his luck could possibly get.

"Elizabeth."

Alexander's voice, strained and almost panicked, lit a fire of worry inside her, and Elizabeth ran from the bathroom, hairbrush still in hand. "Dammit, Alexander," she said as she set the hairbrush on the bedside table and rushed over to him.

With one hand wrapped tightly around the poster and the other arm plastered to his ribs, he wavered on his feet, pain twisting his features. Lowering himself off the platform with a grunt, he blew out a breath. "I'm…afraid I'm—"

"A complete idiot?" Elizabeth accepted his arm around her shoulders, but where he wanted to head for the bath, she glanced back at the bed. "Let me call Roger to help you."

"I dismissed Roger." Alexander leaned heavily on her as they reached the bathroom, then braced himself against the counter, his breathing ragged and shallow.

"You…you did what?" If he hadn't been shot trying to stop her kidnapping, she would have been tempted to grab the hairbrush and beat him with it. "Your surgeon hasn't even cleared you to get out of bed on your own yet, and I find you doing just that, *and* firing the nurse who's supposed to help you? I could rummage in that cabinet of yours and tie you down, you know? You're not currently strong enough to stop me."

She punctuated her harsh words with a gentle hand to his stubbly cheek. The lump in her throat made her next words thick and awkward. "I love you, Alexander. And seeing you go back into the hospital because you were too proud to accept help and tore your stitches is a terrible thing to make me worry over."

"I'm sorry, *chérie.*" Alexander tried to straighten, winced, then blew out a breath. "I didn't think such a short trip would be so...taxing. I simply wanted a shower."

Elizabeth raised a brow. The motion tugged on the still-healing scar over her left eye. "You're lucky I know how that feels. But you couldn't have waited for me to come help you?"

"I'm perfectly capable of getting out of bed on my own," he replied.

"Clearly."

"Blast it, I got a bit dizzy. I seem to remember you trying the same sort of move not long ago." He wrapped his arms around her, holding her gently, and she laid her head on his shoulder.

Five days of stubble scraped against her cheek. "Well, then it seems we're a good match for one another," she said quietly. "But I'm still tempted to tie you to the bed."

Alexander chuckled, then drew in a sharp breath. "I love you, Elizabeth. Now that I'm upright, I think I can manage a shave on my own. Then, perhaps, you'll join me for the shower? After all, how else will you be able to ensure I don't get dizzy again."

Between Alexander's tone and the hard bulge pressing against her hip, she had a pretty good idea what he had in mind—and it wasn't just a shower. "Oh, I'll shower with you. The rest of your plan? Nope. No sex until the doctor clears you."

Elizabeth drew back, eyeing him critically, taking in the scruffy beard, the unkempt hair, and the dark circles under his eyes. He hadn't been sleeping well. The pain woke him multiple times each night, but she'd given him an ultimatum the night before: take a painkiller or she was sleeping in the guest room. With his *control freak* tendencies, he'd relented so he didn't have to let her out of his sight.

"Do you know how hard it's been sleeping next to you and not taking you? Damn the pain. You are mine, *chérie*, and I intend to have you today."

A blush colored Elizabeth's cheeks. Under her chemise, her nipples tightened to hard nubs and a warmth bloomed in her belly. "We'll see about that. Do you need help shaving?"

"No. But I will be a few minutes. Ring Samuel and have him bring up coffee?"

"I'll go get it."

"Elizabeth." The edge to his tone reminded her of how he always spoke during their play. She welcomed the return of his strength, and stopped in her tracks at the bathroom door.

"Yes?"

"Ring Samuel. There's no need for you to deal with something I pay him handsomely for."

With a grimace, she turned and headed for the house phone next to the bed.

"Yes, sir?" Samuel answered on the second ring.

"Um, it's Elizabeth. Alexander asked me to have coffee sent up?"

"Of course, miss. Breakfast too?"

"Not yet. Uh, thanks." Dealing with Alexander's staff— hers now too, she assumed—had left her feeling unbalanced, but at least Samuel, Donatalla, Thomas, and Milos were all patient with her. Of course, she supposed they were paid to be.

"My pleasure, Miss Elizabeth."

Samuel disconnected the call, and Elizabeth sank down

onto the bed. Alexander's majordomo had been especially kind, understanding that she was out of her element living in this huge house with servants and everything she could ever need provided for her.

The previous afternoon, he'd found her doing dishes in the kitchen and had gently taken her arm and led her out of the room.

"Miss Elizabeth, there is no need for this. Donatella and I handle these things."

"I don't know what to do," she'd confessed. "I'm going stir-crazy. I've read five books in the past few days. I can't run any more. I've done enough crunches and yoga to kill me, and Alexander doesn't understand that I'm not used to this. If I were still at home—I mean, in my apartment—I'd clean. I'd probably go help Mrs. Durmont decorate for Christmas. But here…I feel…useless."

"Your things should arrive tomorrow," he'd said with a tentative smile.

"My things?"

"Mr. Fairhaven arranged for the moving company to pack up your apartment. Everything has been sorted and labeled. The furniture will be put in storage until you decide what you want, but all of the boxes will be here tomorrow. Perhaps that will help occupy you. I'm at your disposal when you decide what you wish to keep. This house is yours as much as his now, so you should feel free to make a few changes as you see fit."

"Yeah, I don't think that's going to happen."

"Begging your pardon, miss, but why not?"

She laughed. "Samuel, I've lived here all of three days. I'm not going to barge in and start changing things. Hell, I barely know my way around yet."

Samuel's customary knock startled her. She hadn't even

had the chance to retrieve her hairbrush. *My God, the man is quick.* Elizabeth shrugged into her robe and opened the door. "Good morning, miss. Coffee and biscuits."

Samuel set a silver tray with china cups, saucers, a carafe, and an assortment of shortbread cookies on the bedside table. Elizabeth's stomach growled. Though Donatella had tried to get her to eat repeatedly, she'd had little appetite since Alexander had been shot. Seeing him upright and sporting his customary swagger settled her mind and her stomach. "Will there be anything else, Miss Elizabeth?"

Alexander called out from the bathroom, "We'll take breakfast downstairs today, Samuel. Approximately forty-five minutes. I've had about enough of being an invalid. Ring Nicholas for me and see if he's free this afternoon. We have business to discuss."

"Yes, sir."

With a bow, Samuel hurried out and closed the door behind him.

Elizabeth poured two cups of coffee, shoved a cookie into her mouth, and returned to the bathroom. Alexander leaned over the sink, splashing water on his face. "Now, that's more like it."

"Thank you," he said as he accepted the cup of coffee. "I take it my appearance is satisfactory?"

Elizabeth stepped closer. "Quite." She brushed her lips against his now-smooth cheek. "God. I love how you smell."

A quiet chuckle escaped his lips, followed by a sharp gasp. He waved her off when she started to speak. "Laughing still hurts. But don't fret. I'm fine. Let's sit and enjoy our coffee. Perhaps being upright is something best done in small doses. Plus, I'd like to talk to you about something."

With his arm around her shoulders, Alexander moved gingerly as Elizabeth led him to one of the chairs in the corner of the room. "Sit with me?" He patted his leg, but Elizabeth snorted.

"You're not the only one…feeling needy," she said, a little breathless now that the man she loved looked to be on the mend. As she sank into the chair next to him, she couldn't help shifting her hips against the throbbing between her thighs. "What did you want to talk about?"

Over the past few days, they'd spent hours on those silly innocuous conversations all new lovers indulge in—when Alexander had been able to stay awake, at least. Childhoods, hopes, fears, favorite holiday traditions, even Elizabeth's plan to start her own accounting firm after the holidays. Alexander hadn't been able to do much more than sit up in bed. They'd binged-watched *Sherlock*, half a dozen Christmas movies, as well as the latest season of *Doctor Who*. Whenever he'd napped, she'd gone down to his in-house gym and run away the stress.

Alexander took a sip of his coffee and let out a satisfied sigh. "Ben is coming by today."

"What for?"

An indulgent grin curved his lips. "There's an empty suite in the Fairhaven tower. Five floors below the executive level. I thought you might want to consider it for your accounting practice."

Elizabeth's china cup rattled in its saucer, and her heart did a little dance inside her chest. Taking a long sip of coffee to give her time to think, she stared down at her bare feet, her toes digging into the plush carpeting.

"Alexander, there's no way I can afford the rent at Fairhaven Tower. And before you say something like 'you don't owe any rent,' hang on a minute. You're rich. I get that. And I'm trying to get used to not having to buy groceries or vacuum my living room. But you can't expect me to just roll over and let you do everything for me." Alexander's eyes narrowed and a muscle in his jaw twitched as Elizabeth held up her hand. "I'm starting out all on my own. No firm to back me up, no big name to tread on. And that's how I *want* it. If I take an office from you—no matter how much I might want to—everyone's going to talk."

"Let them talk," he said, an edge roughening his voice. "The space is not generating any income now. What does it matter if it fails to generate income with you in it?"

Elizabeth ran a hand through her unruly locks. "It matters to me. What would it rent for? And don't lie to me."

"I would never lie to you, *chérie*. Trust is the foundation for any relationship—but especially ours. The suite typically rents for five thousand a month."

Elizabeth blanched. Was it possible to *hear* the color draining from one's face? The dull roar in her ears said yes. She'd be lucky if she could afford five *hundred* a month. "Then I have to decline the offer."

"Elizabeth," he said as he leaned forward. "Don't make me insist—"

"Insist?" She set her cup down hard enough to slosh coffee over the rim. "I'm yours in the bedroom, Alexander. Well, once you've recovered. But you don't get to control the rest of my life. Remember?"

Alexander pushed to his feet, swayed, then headed for the window. As he parted the drapes, a bright shaft of sunlight illuminated his chiseled body. He'd lost weight this week, and his skin held a ghostly pallor. A burden had settled on his shoulders, and he leaned his right forearm against the glass, staring out over the Charles River Esplanade.

"I don't want to control your life, Elizabeth," he said quietly. "Just…protect you."

"I don't *need* protection, remember? The…uh…hitman,"

her voice broke as she heard her attacker's voice in her memories once more. Shaking her head, she forced herself to return to the present. "Um, he's dead. No one else is after me."

"Do you know how much I'm worth?" Alexander kept his voice low.

Her brows drew together. "No. You're a billionaire."

"Forty-seven billion."

Holy shit.

Elizabeth reached for her coffee cup again, needing the steadying jolt of caffeine. "That's...how the hell does anyone amass that much money?"

With a weak chuckle, Alexander returned to the chair. His grunt as he sat worried her, as did the expression on his face —something between exhaustion and pain. "A very smart financial planner and shrewd negotiation tactics. But Elizabeth, my point is that someone with my assets is always a target of sorts. I don't often drive myself because from time-to-time, there are threats on my life—on the lives of those I care for."

She reached out for him as her breath started to wheeze in her chest. *Don't panic. Breathe. In and out.* Alexander squeezed her fingers until she got her heart rate under control. "So...Milos..."

"Is a permanent addition to the staff. Thomas—though he was trained as a stunt driver—is also a former army man, and he's a certified black belt in several martial arts. Is there currently danger? No. But there could be. And I would feel much better knowing that you worked in a secure building."

With a nod, Elizabeth released his hand and then started to pace. "I don't even have clients yet."

"You have one." At her confused expression, he continued. "Ben. He used CPH for his accounting. Coincidentally,

9

he paid them approximately five thousand a month. He was as shocked as anyone when you told him what was going on, and now, the only person he trusts with his accounting is you."

"You couldn't have had Ben call me himself? Why do I have to find this out through you?" She snatched another cookie from the tray, stared at the buttery disc, then decided she couldn't possibly eat anything at the moment.

Alexander leaned forward, a slight grimace tightening the corners of his eyes. "I thought it might be easier coming from me. It never crossed my mind that you might be upset or insulted. Sometimes, Elizabeth, you're in the right place at the right time and things simply work out. Why does this have to be anything other than kismet?"

More than once since they'd met, Elizabeth had found herself in the right place at the right time. Even when falling outside of CPH's offices over a month ago.

If she hadn't met Alexander, CPH's plan to set her up for the tax fraud would have worked. No one would have saved her from the hitman. She'd be dead, and Alexander would be alone.

"You'll rent it to me for the full amount?" Shoving the cookie into her mouth, she watched his expression change from frustration to guarded hope.

"I'd prefer to give you a discount. Hell, I'd prefer to give it to you for free, but I'll accept a lease agreement. Perhaps twenty-five hundred?"

"Four thousand."

"Three. For six months. With the stipulation that if your net profits rise above ten thousand dollars in a month for three consecutive months, your rent will increase to four thousand."

"You have a lot of confidence in me."

"I do." He grinned, sensing he was about to win.

Elizabeth rolled her eyes. "Fine." Holding out her hand, she offered to shake on the deal, but Alexander pulled her into his lap and claimed her mouth.

"Shite, Elizabeth. I have missed you. Shower. Now."

2

*D*octors be damned. Alexander couldn't stand another minute without taking his sweet sub. Though he'd only been shot five days ago, he'd spent almost every minute in a bed since then and it had tried his patience. Elizabeth's long blond hair swung over her breasts as she stooped to remove her black lace panties, and he stifled a groan. While he'd been stuck in the hospital, unable to even get out of bed on his own, they'd had a talk about birth control, and he was looking forward to dispensing with the condoms and feeling her wrapped around his bare cock.

"You're sure about this?" she asked.

"Yes. Both the shower and the sex. If I have to go one more hour without taking you, Elizabeth, I may not survive it." Alexander grinned and stepped into the river rock and glass enclosure. He angled the shower heads away from his chest and turned on the spray. Delicious heat washed over his legs. Turning, he let the water sluice down his back. It stung a bit when it flowed over the small wound under his arm, but he cared little. Elizabeth joined him, her nipples tight, dark pink buds. The scent of her arousal mixed with the steam.

"Turn around and put your hands on the bench," he ordered. "Do not move." He'd ached to do this with her for weeks. While he wanted to have her bound, her arse reddened by his flogger, all he could do currently was something of the vanilla variety.

Her heart-shaped arse rose, and he palmed her cheeks, warming them. A shudder went through her. When he slid his fingers down to her folds, she whimpered. "Oh yes, *chérie*. This is how I wanted you. So tight and wet that you will come with only the barest of touches. But you cannot. Do you understand?"

"Uh-huh," she said, fighting for control, thighs trembling, as he stroked her clit. He slapped her right arse cheek as hard as he could muster and was rewarded with a stab of pain through his ribs. A tiny whimper made the move worth it.

"What do you want?"

"You," she begged. "Please."

Alexander used her essence to slick his index finger, sliding it in and out of her at such a languid pace that she tried to encourage him by pushing her hips closer. "One, Elizabeth. I told you not to move."

She stifled a retort and a moan and stilled her hips. "Hurry," she said. "I can't hold on."

"Yes, you can." Alexander replaced his index finger with the tip of his cock. The hot water pounded his back. Slowly, torturing them both, he slid inside. "Shite," he said, "I've dreamed of how perfect you'd feel without a condom, *chérie*, but it was never this brilliant."

The finger he'd slicked with her essence found its way to her arse and swirled around the darkened rosebud. He longed to have her there, too, and she'd agreed to try once he'd recovered. Fondling her clit with his other hand, he slid deep. "Can't," she said, her voice ragged. "Please."

He'd save more play for later when he wasn't in danger of passing out. Now his sweet sub deserved to come. She'd been so strong the whole time he'd been in the hospital, so patient with his inability to get himself out of bed or stay awake for more than a few hours at a time. She deserved all he could give her and more.

With a hard thrust, he tweaked her clit between his thumb and forefinger. "Come now, Elizabeth."

One more pinch of the swollen nub and she flew apart, clenching around his cock like a vise. He pumped in and out of her, moving his hands to her hips where he held her still, not caring that she thrashed about so very much during every release. His name tore from her lips, and his balls tightened, heat shooting up and rocking his entire body.

His vision went white. Waves of pleasure mixed with the pain across his chest. He panted, fighting to regain control of his breath as his fingers tightened on her hips, holding her against him, as much for his own support as hers. "Bloody...hell."

"Alexander." Elizabeth reached a hand back to stroke over his fingers. "Let go."

Spots swam in front of his eyes, but he managed to focus on her creamy skin, the scent of sex that surrounded them, and the pain started to subside. He withdrew with a groan and staggered back against the shower wall. Elizabeth laid a warm hand against his cheek and looked into his eyes. "That wasn't smart."

"I think it was quite brilliant," he replied with a weak grin. "I intend to wear something other than pajamas today and the near-permanent stiffy I've had for the past week would be quite inconvenient with pants."

"A stiffy?" Elizabeth laughed so deeply that her entire body shook. "There are days you are simply too British."

"Keep laughing, *chérie*. I've heard too little of that these past few days." Recovered, Alexander slid his arm around Elizabeth's back, pulling her to his uninjured side and letting the water wash over them. He loved the feel of her against his skin, the way her breath quickened and her lips parted from arousal. He couldn't wait until he could have her in his silks again. Unfortunately, that would have to wait at least another few days. He could barely raise his left arm above his shoulder yet, and he wouldn't bind her unless he could support her weight. He fully intended to blindfold her tonight and see if she'd be amenable to sucking his cock, but she'd have the full use of her arms and legs while she did so.

Now, worry settled in her deep blue eyes. "Are you sure about this?"

He backed her up under the spray. She tipped her head, eyes fluttering shut. A low moan escaped before she got a hold of herself, and Alexander chuckled. She raised her head and narrowed her gaze. "You know I only love you for your shower, right? And for the thousand thread count sheets."

"You're a terrible liar, Elizabeth."

She ran her hands through her hair, causing her breasts to lift and her nipples to tighten. Alexander dipped his head and swirled his tongue around one rosy bud. "Oh God." She held onto his arms, her short nails digging in to his biceps. "We can't. Not again."

With some difficulty, he straightened. "You're probably right. But later…" he promised.

"Oh, yes."

Alexander tried not to let Elizabeth see how much pain he was in as she applied fresh bandages and then helped him dress. His cock didn't want to cooperate, and Elizabeth's exasperation didn't help. Whenever she was frustrated with him, her brows scrunched in such a way, he ached to touch her and smooth the furrows, which just sent him spinning under a fresh wave of arousal. Despite the pain, he felt mostly human for the first time since he'd been shot, and sex with her had only intensified his need.

"Are you sure you want to deal with the stairs?" she asked.

Not really, but I won't be trapped here another minute.

"Yes."

He certainly couldn't meet with Mark Joont, a reporter from WGBH in the bedroom *or* the upstairs study. Over the past few days, when he'd been lucid enough to read the news, he'd grown increasingly worried. All of the major news outlets had picked up the story of his shooting, and Nicholas had been out of the public eye as well—probably spending most of his time at the tables.

When their father had died, Fairhaven Exports' stock price had plummeted. Alexander wouldn't risk that now. The Chairman of the Board of Fairhaven Business Group had to be seen as whole and hale.

Elizabeth took Alexander's arm and helped him down the stairs. He tried to mask the pain, but she had to know. Her shoulders stiffened and a muscle in her jaw ticked several times as they descended the twenty-two steps. He wasn't looking forward to the return trip. By the time they reached the dining room, his chest was throbbing and he was short of breath. "Now I know . . . how smokers feel," he wheezed. "A flight of stairs should not wind me."

"That's what you get for being down part of a lung. Is the pain okay?"

"Fading. Don't fret."

Elizabeth poured them both more coffee and forced a smile as she lifted the lid on a tray of flapjacks. She inhaled deeply. "Gingerbread pancakes."

"What now?"

"Gingerbread pancakes. I think Donatella's enjoying cooking for someone besides you," she said with an easy grin. "Did you ever ask her for anything other than poached eggs on toast?"

"I had the occasional omelet," he said, his shoulders hunching defensively. Had he been *that* predictable? Of course he had been. Though Donatella had once worked in Michelin-star restaurant, and her meals were always delicious, he'd always told her not to worry about cooking anything other than simple meals. Now, as his chef bustled into the room with a quiche in her hands and a smile on her face, Alexander realized the truth of Elizabeth's words.

"I experimented," Donatella said as she slid the steaming quiche onto a trivet in front of him. If you'd prefer, I have the water ready for poaching the eggs, sir."

"That smells delicious. Perhaps I've not been adventurous enough, Donatella." Alexander shot her an apologetic look, and she laughed.

"Very well, then. Sweetbreads for dinner?"

He had to stifle his laugh. "Let's not go that far."

With a nod, the smiling chef almost danced out of the room. "Elizabeth, I need to ask you something."

She paused with her fork halfway to her lips, apprehension in her gaze. "You're not going to try to give me an advertising budget or anything, right?"

Alexander covered her free hand with his. "Well, I wasn't..." Her eyes widened, and he squeezed her fingers. "No, I merely wanted to know if..." Leaning closer, he dropped his voice. "Was I that awful to work for?"

"Awful?" Elizabeth set her fork down. "What do you mean?"

"The past few days...Donatella and Samuel have seemed happier." Alexander glanced back towards the kitchen.

With a smile, Elizabeth patted his hand. "They were worried about you. And maybe...you were a little...aloof."

Alexander tried not to cringe. "And I'm not now?"

She stifled her snort behind her napkin. "You've been a lot more relaxed on pain meds." As he dropped his head into his hands, she reached over and rubbed his arm. "Hey, turnabout's fair play. You got to see me all drugged up and concussed."

The scent of the quiche got the best of Alexander, and he reluctantly picked his head up as Elizabeth deposited a slice on his plate—along with a pancake. "Eat. Or I'm calling Terry."

As he dug in—and he had to admit the pancakes were excellent—he watched Elizabeth attack her own breakfast with gusto. "Mark Joont will be here in less than an hour. I hope he won't require much of our time, and I'm sorry we had to do this on such short notice."

"What else was I going to do today besides attempt to keep you in bed—and try to outmaneuver your hands?" Though she grinned at him, a hint of sadness tinged her words.

"Samuel said your things were arriving this afternoon."

Elizabeth waved her hand. "All four boxes of them? They

can wait. Combatting that ridiculous story the *Babbler* ran that you died is a lot more important than that. Samuel keeps putting more clothes in the closet for me, and you've got a better library than I could ever have dreamed of. I can unpack tomorrow if I have to."

"Well, then may I ask you for one more thing today?"

Narrowing her eyes, she nodded.

"May I take you to dinner tonight?"

Her fork clattered to the table. "You're not ready for that yet. Not a good idea."

Frustration tightened his shoulders, despite knowing she only wanted him to rest. "Dinner is almost always a good idea."

"You love that line, don't you?" She sighed. "On one condition."

He raised a brow. "Yes?"

"Dinner only. No sightseeing, no business, and we come home after and watch a movie in bed."

Inclining his head, he tried not to smile. "Agreed." Elizabeth hadn't put any limitations on what could happen after the movie—that is if he could manage to stay awake.

Elizabeth drained her coffee mug. She'd donned a dark red sweater today and it made her blue eyes stand out dramatically against her pale cheeks. At least the circles under her eyes had faded over the past couple of nights, as she'd slept in a proper bed and not reclined in the hospital's hard plastic chair.

"Are there things we shouldn't say to the reporter?"

"Such as?"

"I don't know. I'm not used to this. Being in the public eye. You're…we're doing this because you're news. I understand that. But that's about as much as I understand."

"Unless Ben stops us from answering a question, there is

nothing we cannot say. All I ask is that you let me take the lead in discussing my health. The company has come under fire enough as of late for Nicholas's indiscretions: both his relationship with Candy and his gambling. My hospital stay did nothing for our stock price."

"Is that why you pushed to come home early?" Her eyes flashed and she narrowed her gaze. "Really, Alexander. You could barely walk." Her voice cracked a little, and she busied her unsteady hands by pouring another cup of coffee.

"No. It was not." He leaned forward and captured her fingers, relishing the warmth of her skin. "We both needed to be home, Elizabeth. If for no other reason than being at Mass General was too risky."

"But Milos killed the…hitman."

"He did, yes. And Pastack and Hayes are in jail. But I wasn't going to take the chance that they'd hired someone else. There's still the matter of the photographer you saw at the ice rink. And while the U.S. Attorney's investigator believes he was just hired freelance, I wasn't about to take a single risk with your safety."

Samuel cleared his throat from the doorway. "Miss Elizabeth, you have a visitor."

"Who?" she asked, brows arching.

Samuel's lips quirked in a frown. "Harry Carter."

"Bloody hell. Did you let that tosser in?" Alexander pushed himself up, wincing as the pain stabbed through his chest.

"He's in the foyer, sir. Milos is with him. I assumed you would not want him unaccompanied."

"You're bloody right. Elizabeth, stay here." Anger rolled through him, the need to pummel Harry within an inch of his life at direct odds with the agony currently banding around his ribs.

"Get the hell out of our house, Carter," Alexander snapped. His breath caught in his chest, but he swung his fist into the thin, reedy man's face with a solid crack. Pain radiated across his body and something popped under his arm. A stitch. Or multiple.

Shite.

Carter stumbled, his shoulder hitting the wall. He rubbed the back of his hand over his bloody lip. "I deserved that."

Milos came up behind Alexander and touched his arm. "Sir. Let me show him to the sidewalk. Forcefully."

"By all means," Alexander wheezed, staggering back and leaning a hand against a cherry wood occasional table to keep himself upright.

"Stop!" Elizabeth hovered in the hall, his order to stay put long disobeyed. "I don't want him here any more than you do, but he was exonerated. I'm assuming he's not here to berate me again. He has to know that would be bad for his health," she said with a nod to Milos.

"I want to apologize," Carter said, rubbing his jaw. His tired gaze switched between Alexander, Elizabeth, and Milos. Wrinkled clothes hung off a body thinner than Alexander remembered, and Carter hadn't shaved in several days.

"I want to hear him out." Elizabeth pressed herself to Alexander's side, and he draped an arm around her shoulders, holding her close. To anyone else, he'd appear possessive. Only he knew that he was holding on so he wouldn't topple over. A trickle of warmth made its way down his side. Blood escaping his bandage wasn't a good sign.

"Miss, are you sure?" Milos said.

"Elizabeth, I do not want him here." Alexander glared at Carter. If he could, he'd pound the man into a bloody pulp. Unfortunately, given his current condition, *he'd* be the one who'd end up in the hospital.

"Please," Carter said, bowing his head and lowering his eyes to the floor. "Give me five minutes."

"No," Alexander replied.

"Milos, take him to the parlor?" Elizabeth asked. "We'll be in momentarily."

After a lingering look at Alexander who only managed a weak nod, the bodyguard acquiesced. "Yes, miss."

Samuel took Alexander's free arm, and the three of them made their way slowly into Alexander's office for some privacy. By the time they reached his desk chair, spots danced in front of his eyes and his wheezing was loud enough to frighten River, who'd been curled up on top of his desk. She picked her head up, hissed, and sprinted from the room. When Alexander was seated, Samuel opened his shirt and *tsked*. "Sir, you're bleeding. Put pressure here." He guided Alexander's hand to his side. "I'm going to get some fresh gauze and a new shirt."

"Thank you, Samuel."

"Stupid," Elizabeth muttered, narrowing her eyes at the blood. "Milos is the muscle. You should have told him to punch Carter. Not tried to do it yourself. The only reason I'm not on the phone to your doctor right now is that I'm pretty sure you'd bust another stitch trying to stop me. I'm going to go deal with Carter."

"Not without me."

"Yes. Without you. You don't need to protect me in this house, Alexander. Carter may be an ass, but he's not stupid. He's not going to try anything with Milos in the room. Relax." She bent down and brushed her lips against his. The subtle scent of coffee and gardenia tickled his nose. "I'll be back in few minutes."

Alexander wanted to spring up and go after her, but

Samuel slid past her with bandages and a white dress shirt in his hands. "Sir, I'll have you fixed up in a few moments."

Harry Carter sat stiffly on one of the leather couches. Milos stood between Carter and the door, hands on his hips. The Greek bodyguard was well over six-foot-three and two hundred pounds of solid muscle. A short, black beard covered his lower jaw, and his brown eyes never left Carter's face.

"Carter."

"Lizzie, thank you for seeing me. And please call me Harry." Carter jumped up, caught Milos's stare, and cleared his throat.

"Sit down," Milos said, his voice low and threatening.

"What do you want?" Elizabeth took a seat across from Carter. Nerves had her hands shaking, but she tried to force a mild expression and keep her breathing under control.

Carter tugged at his collar. "I came to make a peace offering."

"You what?" Shock had her forgetting to keep her voice down, and she hoped Alexander hadn't heard her.

"I fired you. I didn't give you a chance to explain. I assumed that you had made a mistake. Several, in fact. That was wrong. I'm afraid my actions have caused you a tremendous amount of pain. You and Mr. Fairhaven both. I regret that. I haven't been sleeping."

Sitting back and crossing her legs, Elizabeth pursed her lips and scrutinized Carter's face. He'd always been a thin, frail man, but now his face appeared downright haggard.

His blue eyes were nearly as bloodshot as hers. "Thank you."

"I'd like to help find you a new job."

"A new...job? I'm sorry, sir—Harry. I appreciate your apology. Really, I do. And I understand that you were duped by Pastack and Hayes as much as I was. But I don't need or want help from you. I'm starting my own practice. I filed the paperwork yesterday. Bennett Accounting will open its doors in January." She couldn't help her small, prideful smile. Ben had brought over the paperwork the previous morning. All Alexander's doing. Despite the pain and the drugs, he'd still been thinking of her.

Carter nodded, a bit of admiration shining in his eyes. "I'm sure you'll be quite successful. You had a non-compete clause with CPH, but perhaps, in lieu of my being able to smooth the way for you with recommendations, you'll accept a gift."

Her eyes narrowed. "I don't think..."

"Your client list, Lizzie. My own lawyer will likely read me the riot act for this, but CPH has been dissolved, and I'm not planning on returning to accounting work in this state. If you agree, I'll have an amended clause drafted and sent to your lawyer giving you permission to contact any of your former clients. If they want to remain with you, I think they should. You did stellar work for us for five years and I'm sorry I never recognized you for it."

"That's very nice of you. Thank you. You can contact Mr. Hetherington. I assume you still know where his office is."

He chuckled. "I think I can find it. You don't tend to forget unpleasant depositions like that one."

"What will you do?" Elizabeth was surprised she cared, but the man *had* just handed her an olive branch.

"I'm retiring. My brother has a small construction firm in

Florida. I'll do his books, get some sun." Standing, he pulled down the lapels of his jacket and cleared his throat. "Good luck to you, Lizzie. Both with your work and with the events in your personal life. Please tell Mr. Fairhaven that I'm sorry to interrupt his convalescence."

"My convalescence is over," Alexander said from the doorway. He tugged at one of his crisp, white sleeves. "I will be working from my home office until after the holidays, but I'm quite well, thank you."

"I suppose I should have known from that punch." Carter worked his jaw and then smiled. "Please excuse my intrusion. I should have called first, but I was afraid, rightfully so it appears, that you wouldn't agree to see me."

Alexander stifled a snort. "You are among my least favorite people, Carter. The only reason I didn't have Milos throw you out is because this whole goddamned mess had a happy ending." He held out his hand and Elizabeth stepped to his side.

"I will be happy to *show* him out now, sir." Milos said as he stepped forward.

Elizabeth held up her hand. "I won't lie to you, Harry. It wasn't good to see you. But I appreciate your offer. And your apology."

Her former employer nodded, slipping past her with a resigned sigh. "Merry Christmas, Lizzy."

3

"Sir, Mark Joont is here."

Alexander rubbed the back of his neck as he pushed away from his computer. Lying down would have been smarter than trying to work, but there was the matter of the twenty-two steps up to the bedroom—and back down again—and the rest of the Board of Directors needed reassurance that he wasn't at death's door. He'd avoided everyone until yesterday afternoon when he'd finally felt well enough to speak to his admin, Philippa, and tomorrow, he'd have to go into the office for a few hours.

"Where is Elizabeth?"

"I'm right here." She hovered in the doorway behind Samuel. "I was unpacking."

Alexander couldn't help his smile. "Then let us go prove that I am very much alive."

The walk to the parlor felt like a mile, and Alexander refused to let Elizabeth take his arm. Not with a reporter waiting for them. Ben, who'd shown up only minutes earlier, sat next to Mr. Joont, and both men stood when Alexander and Elizabeth entered the room.

"Mr. Fairhaven, it's good to see you up and about," Mark said as he extended his hand. "Miss Bennett."

Once they'd taken their seats and Samuel had served them all coffee, Mark pulled a tape recorder from his pocket. "May I?"

Alexander nodded. "Of course."

The reporter's brown eyes flicked from Alexander to Elizabeth. "I have questions, but perhaps you'd like to start by telling me what happened to lead the *Beantown Babbler* to speculate about your death."

"The *Babbler* is a second-rate gossip magazine that cannot perform the most basic of research," Alexander said. "I was shot when a paid assassin tried to abduct Elizabeth from the restaurant where we were dining. At Mass General, I underwent surgery for a punctured lung. My doctor discharged me after three days, and I've been home for another three days since. As you can clearly see, Mr. Joont, I'm recovering quite well. I've returned to work—though I'm taking meetings from home today. One of the perks of being the boss, after all."

"So you're feeling good?"

Alexander smiled, the practiced expression second nature to him after years in the boardroom. "I'm quite hale, and I've been cleared to resume my daily activities. I can only assume that since I haven't made a public appearance since the shooting, the *Babbler* decided to resort to libel in a pathetic attempt to garner attention."

"Your Board of Directors neglected to return my calls."

"They're paid quite well not to. We have a PR department for such things."

Mark flipped to another page in his notebook. "Fair

enough. What about you, Miss Bennett? Are you well? You were injured in the attack?"

"I'm fine. I sprained my wrist. A bullet grazed my thigh, but it was really only a scratch." She twirled her wrist in a circle. "I'm afraid you have nothing salacious to report on, Mr. Joont."

"The last time we spoke, at the press conference outside your home, you had to refute domestic violence allegations. I've learned that you've since moved out of your apartment and are, presumably, living here. Is that correct?"

"I will never understand this fascination with my relationship status," Elizabeth said quietly. "Yes. Alexander asked me to move in with him and I said yes."

"Will you be saying yes to another question soon?" Mark asked with a sly smile as his gaze skittered to Elizabeth's ring finger.

Alexander choked on his coffee. "That, Mr. Joont, is a private matter," he managed, reaching for a napkin. He dabbed at his lips. "I love Elizabeth. You can report that if you must, but that is the extent of the deeply personal questions we'll answer. Our relationship is between the two of us."

"You're heir to a rather large fortune, Mr. Fairhaven. Not to mention your own personal net worth. You can't tell me your relationship status isn't news. Or something your Board of Directors would want to know about."

Ben cleared his throat. "Is there some speculation that Mr. Fairhaven is hiding his relationship? Or that the Board has raised a single concern?"

At his side, Elizabeth tensed, and Alexander laced their fingers as he cut Mark off before he could reply to Ben's question. "I don't appreciate the tenor of these questions. You're in our home, insulting Elizabeth. If you must know, *I* pursued her. *I* asked her to move in with me. And now, I'm warning you to end this line of questioning right now or I will end this interview."

Alexander refused to look away, pinning Mark Joont under his stare. The reporter stammered for a moment, then cleared his throat. "Let's move on, then. Shall we talk about the case against Phillip Pastack and Leonard Hayes?"

"There's not much to say," Ben offered. "Miss Bennett and Mr. Fairhaven have given their depositions. Both men have pleaded guilty and their sentencing hearings are set for tomorrow."

"That's awfully quick, isn't it?" Mark cocked his head.

"Pastack has less than three months left. He's dying of cancer," Elizabeth said quietly.

Alexander squeezed her fingers. "The judge made an exception because of his illness. He'll live out the rest of his days in a prison hospital. The cases were linked, and in order to sentence Pastack, Hayes had to be sentenced as well. Elizabeth and I will not be attending. We hope to put this whole unpleasant experience behind us and have a happy Christmas."

"Can you share any information about the attempted kidnapping?"

Elizabeth looked at Ben. Once he nodded, she sighed. "I'll give you the high-level version. Pastack was angry that I'd escaped the attempt on my life at my apartment and had managed to formally accuse the firm of tax fraud before they could arrange to have planted evidence against me 'discovered.' The case was open and shut. He—" she shuddered, "—admitted that his plan was to have me die in a very painful way for the trouble I'd caused."

"And he hired the hitman."

She lifted a delicate shoulder. "Yes. I was headed to the ladies' room when the…hitman…grabbed me and forced me out of the restaurant. Only Alexander and my private security stopped him from abducting and killing me."

Alexander felt Elizabeth tremble at his side. He'd had quite enough of this semi-public show. As Mark opened his mouth to ask another question, Alexander held up his hand. "I'm sorry, Mr. Joont. I'm afraid that's all for today. I have a business meeting to attend to."

Elizabeth schooled her features while they exchanged pleasantries, but as soon as the front door shut, she pulled away from Alexander. "I need some air. I'm going for a walk."

"Elizabeth, I put no stock in his rude and baseless implications,"

She forced a smile. "I know. And I love you for that. But he's just asking the questions everyone else will. How can this possibly look to anyone who doesn't know us?"

"Fuck them. What we have is between the two of us. No one has the right to judge our relationship."

"You don't understand," Elizabeth said as she balled her hands into fists and shuddered just out of his reach. "You've been dealing with the press, with gossip, with being in the spotlight for years. I've had…two and a half weeks of it?" Starting to pace, she shook her head. "You can afford to ignore gossip. I can't. I'm starting my own business. In your office building. All anyone's going to say about me for the foreseeable future is that I 'bagged a rich one.'"

She headed for the hall, Alexander striding after her. At the front door, Samuel was at the ready with a wool coat she'd never seen before and fur-lined gloves.

"You promised me you wouldn't give up on us," Alexander said as he caught her wrist.

Elizabeth froze, the coat clutched in her free hand. With a sigh, she turned, her eyes swimming with unshed tears. "I'm not running away. But right now, this house feels like a gilded cage, and I need some air. I'll be back in an hour. I promise."

When she slipped out the door, Milos followed.

Nick let his phone to go voicemail. He didn't need another call from the Forlano family today. Not until he could liquidate some more of his assets. Perhaps he should move. A smaller home, farther from downtown.

An alert flashed across the screen. *Dammit.* Fairhaven Exports' stock had taken a nose dive today with the reports of his brother's demise. Rather than call Alexander—or Ben Hetherington, one of his college roommates and Alexander's lawyer—Nick shrugged into his wool coat, tugged on gloves, and headed out into the snowy afternoon. A walk would clear his head. And perhaps give him some perspective.

4

As Elizabeth stalked down the street, her boots slid on the snow-covered sidewalk. Milos caught her elbow, righting her at the end of the block. Without a coat, hat, or gloves, the massive Greek bodyguard had to be freezing.

"Shit. I'm sorry, Milos. We…can go back." With a sigh, Elizabeth stopped. She hadn't accounted for her bodyguard following her everywhere, but as she glanced around the empty street, a shiver ran through her. She'd not been outside, save for the few brief moments between the hospital and the house, since the hitman had tried to kidnap her. "Or…at least somewhere warmer. Though I don't even have my wallet. I wasn't really thinking when I left."

Buzzing from Milos's pocket stopped her from further apologies. "Yes?" the big Greek bodyguard said. "Of course." He tucked the phone back in his pocket and gestured to an awning in front of a bank's ATM vestibule. "Thomas is coming with the car."

"It's all of three blocks," Elizabeth said, shocked.

"I didn't suggest returning home, Miss Elizabeth. Perhaps

to Miss Kelsey's? Or Miss Toni's?" Milos offered a small smile.

A black town car pulled up alongside them, and Thomas hopped out, his eager brown eyes twinkling. He opened the back door and gestured inside. "Where to?"

Elizabeth furrowed her brow. This...wasn't the limo. Alexander hadn't said anything about the new town car—then again, he'd been largely asleep the past few days.

"I figured you would rather this than the limo. That's Mr. Fairhaven's bag," Thomas said.

With a weak chuckle, Elizabeth nodded, ducking inside the warm car. "Oh, Alexander," she whispered. Her purse, phone, and wool hat rested on the seat. Milos folded himself in front next to Thomas, then they both turned to her.

"Where to, Miss Elizabeth?" Thomas asked.

"Um, Copley Place? It's only four days until Christmas. I suppose I should do some shopping."

Three hours later, with a spa gift basket for Toni and a leather-bound journal for Kelsey, Elizabeth handed her credit card to the liquor store clerk for the eighteen-year-old bottle of scotch for Nicholas. Terrance's gift—a pair of buttery leather gloves—would be delivered the next day.

All through her shopping trip, Milos had remained an unobtrusive presence, though when she'd lost sight of him once or twice, and had started to panic, he'd appeared at her elbow within a breath or two.

Once she'd returned to the car, Thomas grinned. "Where to now, miss?"

"I don't have anything for Alexander," she said. "What do you get for the man who has everything?"

"If you'll allow me, miss. My girlfriend found this neat little shop that she drag—err, brought me to last week. It's a little coffee shop that sells all sorts of local artists' work. You'll want something unique?"

"Yes. And I could really go for a coffee. Let's go."

As Thomas pulled out of the parking lot, Elizabeth leaned forward. "Tell me about her?"

"Pardon?" Thomas gave her a brief glance as he merged with the traffic. Milos sat silently, his dark eyes scanning the street and routinely flicking to the rearview mirror.

"Your girlfriend. How long have you been together?"

"Two years. She lives in Burlington. She's a school teacher."

Elizabeth smiled. His whole face lit up when he talked about his love. "What's her name?"

"Mathilda. Mattie for short."

"Does, um, does Alexander give you Christmas off?"

"Yes, miss. I'm spending it with Mattie's family. I think I —" Thomas shook his head, as if he'd said too much, but Elizabeth jabbed the seat gently.

"You can't leave me hanging like that," she teased. "Spill it."

"I think I'm going to propose on New Year's."

Despite her unease—or at least unfamiliarity—with having staff at her beck and call, Elizabeth genuinely liked Thomas, Milos, Donatella, and Samuel. Happiness welled, and she settled back against the seat. "Oh, that's wonderful! Congratulations!"

Milos clapped Thomas on the shoulder. "Good job, man. Got a ring picked out?"

A blush spread up the back of the driver's neck. Under

his black cap, his ears turned crimson. "I'm picking it up on Christmas Eve."

Sparkling holiday decorations hung from every lamp post on a snowy side street. Sun kissed the space between the buildings, bringing the charm of Christmas in Boston front and center. Thomas pulled into a space in front of a little coffee shop. "Artist's Grind," proclaimed the wooden sign, complete with paint brushes, a steaming cup of coffee, and an easel.

"This is it, miss. Good coffee, too." Thomas hopped out to open her door, and Milos stood outside the shop while Elizabeth slipped inside.

"Hi there," a petite woman with rough-chopped, brown curls said from behind the counter. "Coffee?"

"Sure. Quad-shot Americano, no room?" Elizabeth wandered over to the back of the shop, perusing shelves brimming with hand-painted note cards, picture frames, candles, and hand creams. A small collection of metal work drew her gaze. She picked up one of the business cards.

Macdonald Fergerson
Custom Pieces Available Upon Request

"I don't get a lot of quad-shot orders," the woman said. "You want the jolt or you just tired of that weak-assed shit that the bakeries serve around here?"

Elizabeth turned with a snort, and the woman cracked a wide smile. "I like my coffee to be more than flavored water," Elizabeth replied.

"No Americano for you, then. I've got a pour-over that'll blow your mind. If you don't like it, it's on the house. 'K?"

"Sure. This is your shop?" Elizabeth picked up a bottle of essential oil, uncorked the stopper, and inhaled deeply. The fragrance of lavender calmed her.

"Yep. Owned it a couple of years now. Those are all local

artists you're seeing there. Nothing mass-produced. You looking for something special?"

"A gift for my…boyfriend."

The woman studied Elizabeth while she poured a pot of hot water over grounds that she'd spooned into a conical filter. "You look familiar. Been in here before?"

"No. Never."

"Huh. You famous or something?" The owner cocked her head.

Elizabeth gasped, clutching the little bottle of oil to her chest. "N-no. I mean, no. I've been in the news a little lately, I guess."

"Oh shit. You're dating that Fairhaven. The cute one. You're Eliza? Elsa? I don't get a lot of time to watch TV, but I remember seeing a photo of you. You got hurt. Some legal thing."

"Elizabeth." Uncomfortable, she pulled her coat tighter around her body, wondering if she should leave, but the woman gave her a wide smile.

"I'm Devan. So you're shopping for *him?*"

"What can you tell me about this artist?" Elizabeth picked up a delicate picture frame, deflecting Devan's question. The glass gleamed in the spotlights aimed at the shelves. Elegant and simple, a small red heart decorated the lower left corner. Otherwise, the frame was a mix of gray and clear glass, and the perfect size for a desk.

"She's out in Quincy. She also makes candlesticks, napkin rings, and paperweights. I like her. Even if she does go by the name Crystal."

"I take it Crystal isn't her real name?" Elizabeth couldn't help cracking a smile.

"If it is, I've got some oceanfront property in Arizona I could sell you."

With another snort, Elizabeth glanced over at a coat rack in the corner. A brown cashmere scarf hung from one of the hooks. She ran her fingers down the soft material. It would be the perfect complement to Alexander's jacket.

She was about to pick up the picture frame when a tall man came down the back stairs, carrying a set of fireplace tools with a backpack over his shoulder.

"Think these'll sell, sweetheart?" He set the tools on the counter and grabbed Devan in a one-armed hug, planting a firm kiss on her lips.

Elizabeth turned away, making a pointed effort to examine each one of the holiday cards on the rack and give them some privacy.

"Mac, I've got a customer," Devan hissed.

"Sorry," he said with a chuckle. "I can't help myself around you. I've got another couple Christmas tree toppers in my truck. I'll be back down in a few."

"It's safe, Elizabeth," Devan called. She pushed a steaming cup of coffee towards Elizabeth and then pulled two metal picture frames out of the backpack Mac had left on the counter.

"Those are wonderful," Elizabeth said, gesturing to the frames. "He made those? Mac?"

"Yeah." Devan smiled and straightened her shoulders. "Owner's prerogative. Stocking her boyfriend's art."

"How much?"

"We've been selling the frames for fifty. The fireplace tools...Mac?" Devan shouted up the stairs. "How much for the tools?"

"One-fifty."

Samuel had said she could decorate. The handles of the tools were reminiscent of silk ribbon, and the idea of giving Alexander something that reminded her of silk, even if it was steel, appealed to her. One of the picture frames had the same fluid detail. "I'll take the tools, that frame, the lavender oil, and the scarf."

"Good choices." Devan beamed. "Here's your coffee. It's a single-origin from Peru. Tastes like hot cocoa."

Elizabeth took a tentative sip. "Okay. You're right. That's awesome. Do you sell the beans too?"

"Yep. You want a pound?"

"Hell, yes."

Once the frame and the scarf were wrapped in tissue paper and the essential oil and coffee beans were tucked in Elizabeth's purse, Devan tallied up the purchases. "That's two hundred and seventy-five."

Elizabeth gulped. She'd spent more today than in the past three months. But Ben had worked some sort of miracle with her landlord to get her deposit back, along with two months' rent. None of the security cameras had been working when she was attacked, and the property management company had settled rather than risk a lawsuit. She handed over her credit card and a twenty-dollar tip.

"Thanks. Merry Christmas, Elizabeth."

"Merry Christmas, Devan."

When Elizabeth slipped into their bedroom, Alexander was stretched out on the bed, fully clothed. Once she'd stowed her bag in the walk-in closet, she slid a hip onto the bed next to him.

"That was a long walk."

"Shut it. You know I wasn't walking. Who called you? Thomas or Milos?"

"I didn't check up on you, Elizabeth." He pushed himself up with a wince. "I sent Thomas after you, yes. But all I asked was that he confirm that he found you and ensure you had your wallet and phone. He did so. Your life is your own, *chérie*. I hope that you'll share it with me. For a very long time. But I make no demands on you other than in the bedroom. Save one."

"What?"

"Don't run from me. Tell me what you need and I will give it to you. Even if what you need is space."

His hand rested comfortably on her knee. Three days in the hospital he'd barely been able to stay awake, and she'd done nothing but stroke those strong fingers, memorize every vein, every hair, the feel of his skin against hers. She loved him, even if she had no idea how they were going to deal with the fact that she was a disowned new business owner and he had more money than a small country. "Today was…too much. Between Christmas, the reporter, Carter… I just needed to get away. But I could have handled it better. Not run out so quickly. Poor Milos didn't even have his coat."

Alexander tugged her against him and threaded his fingers through her hair. "I realize this is all new to you, Elizabeth. It's new to me as well. Worrying over you. Knowing how much it would destroy me to lose you. We'll find a balance. We just need to be patient with one another."

Once the server had opened and poured their wine,

Alexander lifted his glass. "To our first Christmas together. And no more hospital visits for quite some time."

Elizabeth laughed, but he caught the nervous edge to her voice. "No more hospitals."

She'd just set her glass down when Alexander reached for her hand. "Mother has decided to come for Christmas."

"She's going to hate me," Elizabeth said as she tried to pull her hand away.

"Why would you think that?" Alexander tightened his grip, rubbing small circles on the inside of her wrist.

"I have two thousand dollars to my name, I've been disowned, and I nearly got you killed. Why would she like me?" Trembling, she forced down a healthy gulp of Bordeaux.

Alexander slid closer in the intimate booth, taking her hand and holding her palm to his heart. "Mother will love you because I love you. We have a buffer with your friends, Nicholas, and Terrance, so you won't be trapped with her alone. She prefers to stay in a hotel rather than with me when she visits, so we'll still have our privacy."

"How does your mother feel about Candy?" Elizabeth arched a brow as the server delivered their steaks. Shifting the discussion seemed to lighten her mood a bit, and Alexander chuckled, careful not to jar his stitches.

"As it turns out, Nicholas broke up with her, and will be joining us alone. Fortunate news all around, as Mother was *not* happy when she saw an article about Nicholas and Candy's relationship online.

"Oh thank God. I really didn't think I could manage to converse with her a second time."

They shared a laugh, though Alexander set down his knife and fork and gripped the edge of the table when intense pain stabbed his chest. "Perhaps we should find a more serious subject," he said, dabbing at a bit of sweat gathered on his upper lip.

"Do you need to leave? I knew you weren't ready for this. You're pushing yourself too hard."

"I need this, Elizabeth. Time with you, in public, doing...*normal* things. In an hour, we'll be home, in bed, and you can ensure I do nothing but rest."

"Damn right." She leveled a stare at him. "No silks. No sex. Just sleep."

"For now," he said with a wicked grin. "But tomorrow...I have other plans."

5

*F*our hours of wandering hadn't helped Nick's mood. His phone buzzed again, and he gave serious thought to throwing it into the bay. Forlano was demanding payment in increasingly angry tones.

Blast it. He'd been so stupid. Not only for betting well beyond his means, but for borrowing money from the Forlano family.

Nick found himself only a few blocks from Ben's townhouse a little after eight. When the lawyer opened the door, he frowned. "You look frozen."

"Bloody close. I'm sorry for showing up unannounced, but…"

Ben stepped back and welcomed Nick into the warm, masculine space. "Your company's better than reviewing legal briefs all night. Drink?"

"Have any tea?" Though the idea of a healthy glass of scotch appealed, Nick needed his faculties tonight to find a way out of this mess.

Ten minutes later, the two men sat in arm chairs around a small fireplace.

"Spill it," Ben said as he took a sip of his merlot.

With the calming scent of chamomile wafting from the mug in his hands, Nick stared into the flames. "I'm in trouble."

"No shit. I hate saying this, but the only reason the press hasn't jumped all over you the past few weeks is that Alexander and Elizabeth have garnered all the news." The lawyer ran a hand through his hair, revealing more gray at his temples than Nick had noticed the last time they'd met for drinks after work.

With a shake of his head, Nick sighed. "I owe the Forlano family a…significant sum."

"Define significant." Ben set his glass on a side table, then leaned forward.

"A little under a million. But with the interest…by the time I can liquidate enough assets to pay them…it'll be well over."

The color drained from Ben's face. "Fuck."

"What do I do?" Nick's voice cracked as he stared into the flames. "Forlano's called me six times today. I can get him a couple of thousand, but that's not going to hold him off for long."

Ben shook his head. "Get him whatever you have, man. And grovel. Get him to agree to a payment plan."

Snorting, Nick rolled his eyes. "They don't believe in payment plans."

"Then I only see one choice, Nick. You've got to go to Alexander."

Elizabeth woke on the twenty-third to half a dozen text messages from Toni, threatening to go find that reporter from WGBH and send her whole Italian family after him. The Grimaldis didn't have anything to do with the mob—anymore—but Toni claimed an uncle or two still knew people.

As she read the story, she struggled not to cry. No, Mark Joont hadn't come right out and accused her of being a gold digger, but the comments on the online article did. Alexander, once he'd calmed her enough that she wasn't on the verge of another panic attack, headed into his downtown office to speak to Ben and Philippa about how to spin the negative press—and put in a physical appearance to dispel any lingering rumors of his ill health.

Alone, desperate for a distraction, she closed herself in the guest room with all of her boxes. The meager remnants of her former life did little to assuage her nerves, though. If anything, being reminded of how little she'd had while sitting on luxurious carpet, surrounded by the finest furniture, and drinking coffee out of a bone china cup made things worse.

Samuel knocked, and Elizabeth swiped at her cheeks. "Come in?"

"Miss Elizabeth? You have a phone call." Samuel held out a cordless phone.

No one she knew had Alexander's—hers now too, she supposed—home phone number. "Who is it?"

His dark eyes shifted to down to his feet. "The woman identified herself as your mother. She is not happy."

Why now?

For more than five years, she'd tried to forget. But now, the pain and betrayal rushed back like a tidal wave. "H-how did she get this n-number?"

Samuel scowled, and shaking his head, he ground out, "She called Mr. Fairhaven's office. Philippa's assistant passed along the information."

"Lovely." Her hand trembled as she reached for the phone.

"Do you wish me to stay?"

Meeting Samuel's gaze, Elizabeth tried to force air into her lungs. Her throat constricted painfully. Pressing her free hand to her chest, she nodded. "Please," she wheezed. "Dammit."

Samuel knelt down and laid his hands on her shoulders. "Breathe. In and out."

"Try-ing."

"You can always hang up on her." Samuel cracked a small smile. "Or I could. Or we could leave her on hold for an hour and hope she hangs up of her own accord."

Elizabeth managed half a chuckle. "No. I have to do this." She took a deep breath, and though a hint of wheezing remained, her lungs obeyed her command. Sitting among the boxes that represented her life, she leaned an arm on a stack of books and punched the hold button. "H-hello?"

"Lizzie. What were you thinking?"

Her mother's harsh voice startled Elizabeth, and the shock sent her heart rate shooting up again. "Excuse me?"

"My daughter is not a two-bit hussy who shacks up with a playboy in order to get ahead in life." Elizabeth leaned forward, tucking her head between her knees. Only her desperate need to hide her panic from her mother kept her upright. "Well?" Avery asked.

Picking her head up, Elizabeth tried to channel her anger.

"Mother, I have not 'shacked up' with Alexander. I happen to love him. And before you say another word, I'm not your daughter. Not anymore. You made that very clear when you disowned me. The only reason you're calling now is because you think I'm going to tarnish the family name."

Avery's voice softened. "I care about you, Lizzie."

"Bullshit."

"Language!"

Elizabeth rolled her eyes, the memories of their last conversation steeling her. "Oh, fuck it, Mother. I'm an adult and if I want to swear, I'm going to swear."

"You had the perfect life, Lizzie. A loving fiancé, a good job. And then you had to go to the press and air our dirty laundry." All the judgement returned with a vengeance.

The perfect life. Under the thumb of an abusive fiancé.

"How's Darren?" Elizabeth didn't really care about him, but she secretly hoped that her ex-fiancé wasn't still part of the 'family.'

"He's head of cardiology, now. Had you not decided to throw your life away, you'd be a very powerful woman." The words grated, but she shouldn't have been surprised.

Her bitter laugh held no mirth. "Powerful? You and Darren controlled everything I did, everything I said, everything I thought. I'm glad you found the child you always wanted, Mother. Marry him off to some socialite and you'll have the perfect family. I'm done with this conversation. And with you. If you speak to Dad, tell him I love him. Goodbye."

Elizabeth ended the call and barely noticed when Samuel eased the phone from her hand. "Miss?"

"I'm okay," she mumbled, looking up at him and seeing concern in his dark eyes and pursed lips. "I don't ever want to speak to her again." Elizabeth tried to force some strength into her tone, but her words escaped as more of a plea than an order.

"I will convey that message if she calls in the future. What about your father?"

"He'll never call. He's written me off." Tears balanced on the edge of her lids. In the corner of the room, the Christmas tree reminded her of happier times as a child. Climbing into her father's lap and opening presents, smelling his once-a-year Christmas cigar, watching him assemble her Dream House, her first bike.

If only her father had been a stronger man. Or if she'd been a better daugh—no. She'd been a fine daughter. Her parents should have been better.

"Come have some tea, miss." Samuel offered her his hand, and she took it, letting him guide her down the hall and into the upstairs study. She loved this room. The heavy draperies were pulled back to reveal Boston blanketed in snow. Elizabeth sank down onto the chaise and pulled a throw around her body. Chilled, she let out a few hoarse, choking sobs as the tears plopped into her lap.

"Shall I call him?" Samuel asked softly when her sobs had quieted and she'd caught her breath.

"No. I have to deal with this on my own," she said, wiping away the tears. "I hadn't thought about them in years and all of a sudden, it's like I'm right back in Seattle. Parents are supposed to love their children. Support them. Not…" She didn't know why she was confessing all of this to Samuel. But he was easy to talk to and he didn't judge. "Thank you, Samuel. I'm fine. Really." Forcing a smile, she looked up at him and nodded. "I'm going to watch the snow fall for a while. Maybe call Toni and make sure she and Cesario are coming for Christmas. You don't have to babysit me."

"I'll check on you in a bit, miss."

Later that day, Elizabeth called Ben.

"What can I do for you, Elizabeth?" The sound of pages flipping accompanied his distracted tone.

"I need you to draw up a legal document that states that I'm not after Alexander's money. Is there such a thing as a prenuptial without the nuptial part?"

Ben sputtered for a moment. "Wh-where is this coming from? Alexander is certainly not asking you for anything of the kind."

"No. He's not. And he won't. But I want it in writing. I don't want there to ever be a question that I'm with him for what he…can provide me."

"Elizabeth, you will certainly be a wealthy woman in your own right soon. The settlement from your suit against Hayes should be at least three million, and your own work will be lucrative. The Red Sox GM contacted me today. He would like you to continue to handle accounting for the team. I agree that with your projected net worth, and with Alexander's, that an agreement upon marriage would be prudent, to protect both of you, but there is no need for this now."

"You won't help me?"

"Not with this. No. There is simply no need."

Elizabeth rubbed the back of her neck, trying to dispel the headache trapping her head in a vise. "Well, can you at least draw up a will? I want to make sure that if anything happens to me, my parents won't get one bloody cent. They're still my next of kin. Technically."

"That I can do. I'll need the details of any beneficiaries you'd like to name and where you'd like things to go."

Elizabeth settled back at Alexander's desk, closed her eyes, and began to dictate.

Alexander's phone buzzed in his pocket. "Yes?"

"I am at the hotel, where are you?" Margaret Fairhaven's clipped tones had Alexander cringing.

"I am five minutes away, Mother. Traffic is abysmal. There was an accident in the tunnel."

She sighed. "Very well. I'm in the bar."

With a twinge of pain, Alexander tucked the phone back into his pocket. He'd seen his doctor today, and though he'd been chastised for the punch that had popped two stitches, he'd been cleared to resume all of his normal activities, provided his lungs didn't bother him. "Anything you can do to speed this up will be appreciated, Thomas."

The driver met Alexander's eyes in the rear-view mirror. "Yes, sir."

Alexander found his mother in a dark booth at the Fairmont Hotel, sipping a glass of red wine. "Gently, Mother," he said as she embraced him and pressed against his still-healing wounds.

With a concern he hadn't seen in her eyes in years, she patted his hand as they sat. "How are you, Alexander?"

"Sore. But otherwise well. It could have been much worse. My surgeon gave me a clean bill of health this morning." The past few nights, when the pain would wake him, his thoughts would wander to what could have been. His death. Elizabeth's. With a small smile, he fingered the small box in his jacket pocket.

"I know that look," Margaret said. "You're planning something. A proposal? Already? I haven't even met her."

"Not yet, Mother. Elizabeth isn't ready. But a bit of a commitment, nonetheless. I do hope she'll consent to be my wife soon. Before the holidays next year."

"I've read the papers." Margaret nodded at the waiter who took Alexander's order of Macallan, neat. When he'd rushed off, she continued. "You're confident she is not after your money?"

"Yes." He wouldn't dignify his mother's question with any further response.

"You'll be asking her for a prenuptial agreement, then."

"Mother, this is premature. I love her, and she makes me happy. There's not a dishonest bone in her body, and once you meet her, you'll understand that."

"Very well. Is your Elizabeth at least a good conversationalist? After the last time I had to endure Nicholas's…slave for a weekend, I'm afraid I'll say something I'll regret. Not that the poor woman would understand me."

Alexander chuckled. "Nicholas has a gift for all of us this Christmas. He ended things with Candy. That said, Elizabeth is brilliant. I believe you'll like her."

"Well, that is a relief," Margaret said and then took a delicate sip of her wine. "Then the only uncomfortable topic will be his gambling."

"It's Christmas. Can we avoid that unpleasantness for one day?"

"No."

Downing his scotch in a single swallow, he almost signaled the server for another round. His mum had called him the day he'd come home from the hospital. Not only had she chastised him for getting shot, she'd bent his ear for twenty minutes about his brother's financial worries. Alexander didn't remember much of the conversation—so hopped up on pain meds he couldn't think straight—but he knew Margaret intended to sit Nicholas down and give him a proper talking to.

Nicholas still had his flat and his cars, but his disposable income had dwindled to nothing between the money he owed the track and the clubs in Atlantic City. Rumors abounded about the two Fairhaven boys. One dead, the other embroiled with some less-than-savory characters from Boston's North End. No one who valued their lives admitted that the mob still had their fingers in the local gambling scene, but Alexander would bet on that fact.

"Please, Mother. Give us all one day to celebrate being together, alive and well. Elizabeth and I have both invited friends, you're here for the first time in several years, and I'd like to enjoy the day. We can have an intervention of sorts on the twenty-sixth. All right?"

"Very well," Margaret said with a wave of her hand. "But if he makes the news again before Christmas, I may break that promise."

Alexander tried not to roll his eyes or sigh. "I should go. Elizabeth is expecting me for supper. If you'd like, you could join us?"

Margaret's blue eyes softened. "Any other night, I'd take you up on that, love. But I've been up for eighteen hours. I'll be busy with my foundation tomorrow—along with some last-minute shopping. You'll have a car pick me up on Christmas morning?"

"Of course. Thomas will be here at eleven," Alexander said as he leaned over to kiss his mother's cheek.

"A mother should not bury her son," Margaret said, her voice a hoarse whisper. "See that I do not have to."

"I will do my best."

6

lizabeth, I'm on my way home. Are you busy?

She smiled as Alexander's text flashed across her screen.

Just finished wrapping presents. Why?

Placing the gifts under the tree, she surveyed her handiwork. Mid-morning, she'd realized that she'd neglected to get anything for Alexander's mother, so she'd had Milos take her back to Artist's Grind where she'd picked up another pound of coffee and a box of handmade truffles, and then had managed to sneak gifts for the staff into her bag as well with a little help from Devan. Gloves for Milos, a nice pen for Samuel, and a local hot cocoa mix for both Donatella and Thomas.

Go upstairs, strip, and lie down on the bed.

With a tiny gasp, Elizabeth glanced around. She was alone, thank God, so no one could see the flames that engulfed her cheeks. Every day, more of the man she knew returned.

Once she'd firmly closed the bedroom door behind her,

she did as he commanded. Already she ached for him. He'd managed a light flogging last night, and she'd lost count of the number of times he'd ordered her to come—three?, four?—before he'd plunged deep inside of her. She used to go weeks without a release, months even, and then only from her vibrator, but now she felt much like a sex-starved maniac half the time.

Her nipples tightened in anticipation, and her sex was already slick with need. As the door opened, Alexander's appreciative purr raised gooseflesh on her arms, and she tried not to shiver.

"I have been looking forward to this all day, *chérie.*" He shed his jacket, tie, and shirt as he stalked towards her, a predatory gleam in his eyes.

She took careful notice of his wounds, pleased the redness was fading. She might be his sub, and she'd agreed to obey him in the bedroom, but she'd put a stop to their play damn quick if she thought he wasn't well enough for the exertion.

Once he'd withdrawn a black silk bag from his cabinet, he approached her. "I have something I'd like to try with you, Elizabeth."

She arched a brow, but before she could answer, he slipped the blindfold over her eyes. "I don't get to see what it is?"

"No, but I'll explain as I go. We won't do anything you don't want to do." Alexander sealed his promise with a kiss that left her breathless, and when fastened the leather cuffs around her wrists, then bound her to the headboard, she tugged at the restraints, testing them.

"I'm going to torture you a little, my sweet sub. Don't come until I say." Alexander bound her ankles wide, then ran his smooth hands up and down her legs. "You are exquisite, Elizabeth." His first kiss to her mound elicited a moan, and he spent what felt like forever lavishing attention over her entire body. Her release threatened as he scraped his teeth over her nipple, receded as he attached the clamps, then tried to pull her under again as he lavished attention on her clit.

"Please. I can't hold on," she sobbed, breathless.

"No?" He asked from between her legs. The barest hint of stubble tickled the sensitive flesh of her inner thighs, and she almost lost her battle for control. "Who am I, Elizabeth?"

"Wh-what?" She sucked in a deep breath, trying to clear her thoughts.

"Who am I to you? What am I?"

Oh God. "My Dom."

His lips were suddenly next to her ear. "What do you want your Dom to do to you?"

"Control my pleasure," she gasped.

"Very good." His tongue swirled around her earlobe and trailed down to her jaw. "I am going to push you, *chérie*. If you need me to stop, you know how."

Ankles and wrists freed, she let him help her stand, then bit her lip as he turned her around.

"You are so luscious, *chérie*. Curvy and soft here." He nibbled her right ass cheek. "Firm and toned here." A breathy kiss to the back of her thigh. His talented fingers dug into the soft flesh of her ass, warming, loosening.

Alexander urged her to bend over the bed, but left her arms free. Elizabeth gripped the thick comforter, anticipating a spanking or perhaps another flogging. Late the previous night, she confessed how much she loved the light stings of pain he could deliver.

"Open for me, Elizabeth." As he tangled his fingers in her hair, she spread her legs, and his cock nudged her drenched channel.

Only a strangled moan escaped as he slid deep, and she

clenched around him, arching her back in pleasure. A noise she didn't recognize—a soft snap—barely registered, but then a cool, wet finger brushed over the rosebud of her ass. Elizabeth whimpered and squirmed.

"Wh-what…?"

Alexander leaned over her, pressing a tender kiss to her shoulder as he thrust deep. "Will you let me play with your arse, Elizabeth?"

"Uh…yellow." She pushed against him, desperate to come, hoping her release would bring some clarity. "Too much…"

Alexander gently rocked his hips back and forth in long, soothing strokes. "Better?"

"Yes." A few tears escaped, dampening the sheets, as Alexander returned his hands to her hips and held on.

"You feel magnificent."

Despite the storm of sensations threatening to carry her away on a wave of overwhelming pleasure, she managed one clear thought. "Try again."

"Try what?" Groaning, he stilled his thrusts, then ran a warm hand up her back. "What do you want, Elizabeth?"

"P-play…with my ass."

"Are you sure? This is like taking my cock, *chérie*. It's nothing I will ever ask you to do unless you're ready and willing."

Elizabeth pushed against his hips, forcing him deeper inside. For that, she earned a quick slap to her right ass cheek. The pain feathered out in delicious waves, and she moaned as she purposely provoked him again. "I'm…sure."

"Say *red* if this becomes too much," he murmured as something cool spread over the sensitive rosebud. He didn't push, didn't try to breach the tight hole, just swirled his finger around and over as he rocked in and out of her pussy.

Elizabeth couldn't catch her breath. The intense arousal mixed with a hint of fear kept her on the edge of release, her body enflamed with passion, every nerve ending exploding at once.

"Please," she begged. "More."

A firm pressure against her ass rocked her to her toes. "Bear down," he commanded her, and dimly aware he wasn't using his finger anymore, she did as he asked, a thrill lancing from her toes to her pussy as something small and hard popped into her ass.

"Oh God," she whimpered. "Yes."

"More?" Alexander thrust hard, and the sensation of being so completely filled in every way had her crying out, nodding, trying to form the words to tell him to push her, to take her over the edge and let her fly.

"Y-yes," she finally managed, and whatever he'd put in her ass started to vibrate. Elizabeth screamed. "Please!"

"Come now, Elizabeth."

Alexander thrust into her, and the tiny vibrator curled her toes as her climax shattered her.

"Oh God, Elizabeth, that's it. Come for me." He groaned and grabbed her hips, driving himself deeper than she thought possible. As he fell with her, she dissolved into nothing but pure, overwhelming ecstasy.

As they lay in bed together, Alexander stroked her back. "I didn't expect you to lose yourself so completely from one, tiny butt plug," he said with a chuckle.

"How long was I...?" She didn't remember the plug

coming out, nor Alexander removing the blindfold or the cuffs. Her skin smelled vaguely like vanilla and citrus, as did he, so he'd obviously administered aftercare without her even knowing.

"In subspace? Perhaps ten minutes. You babbled quite incoherently as I tended to you." He pressed a kiss to the top of her head.

Elizabeth pushed up on an elbow. "You didn't carry me, did you? Your doctor—"

"Shhh. Relax. I didn't carry you. Soon, though. I've missed that." Alexander pulled her closer, letting her rest her head on his shoulder. "A hot washcloth only. And a bottle of water."

"God. I don't remember any of that." Embarrassed, she turned her face to his neck. Have you…done that before?"

"Not often." His voice rumbled in his chest. "No one should attempt arse-play without the utmost trust. One day, perhaps you'll take my cock there?"

Her eyes wide, Elizabeth met his gaze. "You're too big. There's no way…"

A laugh rolled through him, followed by a wince and a curse. "Shite. I'll be happy when that no longer hurts." Alexander shook his head. "We'd prepare you, *chérie*. Larger butt plugs, over the course of weeks or months. Only if you want to try."

Worrying her lip under her teeth, she found only honesty in his eyes. "Maybe. We can at least try…*that*…again one of these days." She nodded towards the now-clean butt plug resting on its silk bag on the nightstand.

"As I've said many times, Elizabeth. You have all the control. I don't care if we're playing ten years from now doing something we've done hundreds of times. You can *always* put a stop to everything with one word." He sealed his promise with a kiss, and she snuggled closer, content to enjoy a quiet moment on Christmas Eve with the man she loved.

As Alexander joined Elizabeth in the shower, he sensed a change in her emotions. "Is something wrong, *chérie?*"

"I have to meet your mother tomorrow. And…did you read the comments on the *Babbler's* story? Opportunistic, gold-digging, desperate… Those were the nicest adjectives." Her eyes shimmered, and Alexander cursed his every dollar as he gathered her close under the hot spray.

Alexander had half a mind to see if he could engineer Mark Joont's termination, and in fact, he'd ranted to his admin several times about it over the few hours he spent in the office today. But Philippa and Ben both confirmed Mark hadn't published anything patently false, and so all Alexander could do was ensure he never gave the reporter preferential access to a story again.

"There are days, Elizabeth, I think the worst of humanity lives in the comments section." He spilled shampoo into his hands and then started massaging her scalp. She sighed as she leaned against him, letting her head tip back. "I'd shield you from all of this—if only I could. I'm afraid it's the danger of being a Fairhaven—or associating with one. I'm sorry if it causes you one moment of grief, and if there's ever anything I can do—"

"My mother called."

"What?" Alexander cursed his harsh tone, for Elizabeth flinched under his touch. Turning her, then brushing a few suds away from her eyes, he cupped her cheek. "When?"

"Yesterday. She wanted to know why I'd shacked up with a playboy to get ahead in life. She implied I ruined the family name with my *gold-digging*. Or would if I didn't end this insanity. Us." Hurt swam in Elizabeth's wide, blue eyes. "She's not the only one who thinks that way. Everyone's going to assume I'm with you for your money. For the clothes, the diamonds I know you never returned to Dorfman's, the roof over my head. The more you *give* me, the more people are going to talk."

"People are going to talk no matter what we do. Even if you stepped out with me wearing that ill-fitting fleece you had on the first night we met, people would gossip. You own no jewelry. I have never known a woman not to own a single pair of earrings."

"And the clothes that keep showing up in the closet?" She pulled away, then reached for the soap.

"Options. As neither of us felt comfortable even leaving the house until a few days ago, having Marjorie send things over was easier. When you feel like shopping for yourself, you can donate anything you don't like."

She sighed as she smoothed soap over his chest, carefully avoiding his stitches. "It's not that I don't like what you've bought me. Or that I don't understand the necessity of it all. I'm just...out of my element."

Alexander wrapped his arms around her and for several long minutes, they let the hot water melt away the strain of the past few weeks.

"Distract me," Elizabeth said as she pulled away, then stepped out of the shower. "How was your day?"

7

On Christmas morning, a light snow fell outside the floor-to-ceiling windows in their bedroom. Alexander dressed carefully—he'd overdone it with Elizabeth the previous evening, but he didn't care. Taking her deep into subspace had been worth it. Another week and these blasted physical limitations would be gone and he'd be able to try a few new things with her—like the deep red hemp ropes he'd wrapped and left under the small tree in their bedroom. He'd found them a private Shibari instructor, and with Elizabeth's permission, he'd have her bound to the St. Andrew's Cross in such a way she'd be unable to move at all while he wrung climax after climax from her.

Brushing some of River's orange fur from his black sweater, he narrowed a gaze at the cat, who *mrrped* happily as she wound around his legs. "Don't go begging me for tuna," he said. "I know for a fact Donatella feeds you."

The cat butted her head against his leg in response.

"Really? She didn't?" Alexander gingerly reached down and scratched behind River's ears.

"She lies," Elizabeth said from the doorway.

"She *is* looking a little round these days." He straightened with a wince and grinned at the woman he loved. Her long-sleeved red dress hugged her curves, and she fiddled uncomfortably with one of the ruby earrings he'd given her this morning.

"Are you ready? Toni and Papa Grimaidi just got here. Kelsey and Nicholas are arguing over a game of chess. Samuel said your mother's driver called and she's ten minutes away. I don't want to have to face her alone."

Two steps and he had her in his arms. "She will love you. But yes, I am almost ready. I only have one thing to do. Sit with me for a moment?"

Her brows drew down and she scowled. "I don't trust you."

"You trust me completely. That's why we're sitting here." He dipped his hand into his pocket and pulled out a diamond bracelet with a platinum heart-shaped clasp.

"No more jewels!" she protested immediately and tried to scoot back on the bed. "I told you—"

Her words died in her throat when he held up his hand. "Do you remember the photo of Candy and me that bothered you so much before we started dating?"

"Of course. I'm glad she found a new Master. For everyone's sake."

"Nicholas doesn't know what he wants right now. I'm not even certain he needs a slave, so much as he needs commitment. Loyalty. Love." Alexander shook his head. "But that's a subject for another day."

"And *that?*" Elizabeth gestured to the glittering jewels.

"Nearly dying puts one's life in harsh relief. I love you, Elizabeth. With all that I am. If I thought you'd say yes, I'd propose this instant."

Her breath hitched. "It's too soon."

"Yes, it is. For you anyway. And so I'll wait. Forever if I have to. Consider this," he laid the bracelet across her wrist, "an interim step. I had this made for you. The clasp locks. The key is in my safe. Would you consider wearing this as a symbol of our commitment? Of our love?"

She worried her lip under her teeth, and he rushed to try to soothe any fears. "If you ever decide I'm not who you want, you need only ask, and I'll unlock it."

Though it just might destroy me.

"Like…a collar. But not," she finally managed, her voice barely above a whisper.

Blast it, he'd made a true cockup of things now. "No." He ran a hand through his hair. "There are two types of collars, Elizabeth. Those who enjoy the role of a slave wear one type. However, just as many Doms consider a collar more of a commitment than anything else. Nicholas—he had that with another woman many years ago. He asked her to wear his collar and she agreed. She was never his slave. She was his sub, his lover, his partner."

"What happened to her?" Elizabeth touched the diamonds gingerly, as if she expected them to burn or cut her somehow.

Alexander sighed. "She fell ill and died five years ago."

"Oh God. Poor Nicholas."

They sat together for several minutes without speaking, Alexander's worry growing with every breath. He'd made a mistake. She wasn't ready. At least not today. Why did he have to attempt this on Christmas Day?

"If I say no…is that like saying *yellow* on our relation-ship?" Her quiet words pierced his frantic thoughts, and he met her gaze.

"No. If you're not comfortable with a symbol of commitment yet, then I'll lock this away until you are. Or forever if you'd prefer a more traditional symbol." Alexander brushed his fingers over where he hoped one day she'd wear a wedding band. "I love you, Elizabeth. I don't want you to ever doubt that. Bracelet or no bracelet."

She cupped his cheek with her free hand. "I don't need diamonds to know you love me."

Alexander slid the bracelet from her wrist, clutching it so tightly, the diamonds dug into his flesh. "I can put—"

With a tender kiss, she silenced him. "I needed to know I had a choice, Alexander. That you wouldn't push me beyond what I was ready for." With a smile, Elizabeth offered him her wrist.

"Yes?" Hope surged.

"Of course." Elizabeth smiled shyly at him. "But no more jewelry. Not unless we…uh…get married. And even then, a ring. Nothing more. Okay?"

As Alexander locked the bracelet around her wrist, he met her gaze. "No more jewelry. I promise."

As she fiddled with the bracelet, Elizabeth marveled at the events that had all conspired to bring them both here, now. Every time she started to fear she and Alexander were too different, he went and did something like this. Something that showed her the type of man he was. Loving. Respectful.

Also demanding. But not in a way that left her feeling less than. He wanted all of her. Body and soul and heart. And God help her, she knew one day she'd marry him.

She'd never intended to leave him before, but somehow,

the idea of wearing his *cuff* made things more permanent. The weight of it, despite how much she wanted to be his, staggered her. And now she had to meet his mother.

Alexander kept an arm around her waist as they made their way down the curving staircase. "Are you making sure I don't run?" she whispered in his ear.

"Perhaps. Relax, *chérie*. Mother does not bite."

A clipped, older British voice reached them from just beyond the foyer. "Nicholas, you are embarrassing the family. Your gambling problem is fodder for all of the papers, and you're damaging the reputation of the entire Fairhaven name. Alexander, for all of his philandering over the years, understands what is expected of him as the head of a multi-billion dollar corporation."

Alexander stopped Elizabeth on the bottom step. "Wait here," he said, brushing a light kiss to Elizabeth's cheek. His anger pulsed in the set of his shoulders and his clenched fists.

"Mother, we agreed. Today is not the time for this," he said sharply.

"*Et tu, Brute?*" Nicholas asked. "You couldn't have warned me?"

Elizabeth peered around the banister, catching Alexander shaking his head. "I have. More than once. We'll discuss this —the three of us—tomorrow."

Margaret Fairhaven turned, caught sight of Elizabeth, and offered a tight-lipped smile. "Well, don't be shy."

As Elizabeth approached, Alexander held out his arm so he could pull her to his side. "Mother, this is Elizabeth Bennett."

"It's a pleasure, Mrs. Fairhaven," Elizabeth said as she offered her hand.

"Margaret, please." The elder Fairhaven narrowed her blue eyes as she caught sight of the diamonds around Elizabeth's wrist. "I could use a glass of Champagne, and you, Elizabeth, look like you're about to topple over. Shall we move to the parlor?"

"*Chérie*, champagne?" Alexander pressed a fluted glass into her hand. She turned, forcing a smile for him. His emerald green eyes darkened, and when he wrapped his arm around her, she settled slightly.

"To family and new friends," Alexander said as he lifted his flute.

Elizabeth touched her glass to his, then Margaret's. The rest of the group—Toni, Papa Grimaldi, Kelsey, Terrance, Ben, and Nicholas—gathered around them. The bubbles slid down her throat—a throat still raw from the screams Alexander had coaxed from her the previous night.

"Are you named after Austen's Elizabeth?" Margaret asked when they'd all taken seats around the fire.

Elizabeth's voice cracked. "My m-mother loved that book."

"Are you as strong as she was?"

"Yes, Mother. She is. And like her namesake with Darcy, Elizabeth also rejected me many times," Alexander said as he rubbed Elizabeth's thigh.

Nicholas chuckled, and Toni, Kelsey, Ben, and Terrance stifled their own snickers. Papa Grimaldi cleared his throat. "Elizabetta is a smart woman," he said in heavily accented English. "Maybe she reject you so you prove your worth."

This time, everyone laughed, even Margaret. "Signore

Grimaldi, if that was not the reason, I will lose a healthy dose of respect for my son's love."

I didn't understand why he'd want to bother with me. Elizabeth looked down at the new black heels that had found their way into her closet. Nothing she was wearing today was hers. At least not from before Alexander. Despite his insistence that she belonged with him, and the connection they shared, she still felt like an impostor in these new clothes and jewels. She'd paid for the manicure herself, at least.

Sun streamed through the large windows, illuminating a winter wonderland outside. Glittering pillows of snow in the backyard drew Elizabeth's gaze. As the small group engaged in conversation, Elizabeth took her second glass of champagne, delivered by Samuel, and wandered over to the Christmas tree. Of the four trees in the house, only the one in the upstairs study showed any real personality—she and Alexander had both added their personal touches over the past few days—but the tree in front of her was real and smelled like the holiday should. She turned and watched her family—new and old—get to know each other. Scents of goose, roasted potatoes, and stuffing wafted in from the kitchen.

Margaret approached and touched her arm. "I would like a moment, dear."

Elizabeth looked to Alexander, pleading silently for him to intervene, but he was engaged in a lively bit of banter with Papa Grimaldi about the best cannoli in the North End and didn't notice her distress. Margaret, however, did.

"I don't bite. Nor am I interested in stuffing your body in the laundry chute. I simply wish to have a bit of a chat about my son."

Nerves swirled in her belly, but she allowed Margaret to

pull her into Alexander's downstairs office, where the older woman shut the door behind them.

"Alexander has never introduced me to one of his romantic interests before," Margaret said, taking a seat in one of the guest chairs and inviting Elizabeth to join her. "He loves you. Do you feel the same towards him?"

"Yes."

"And you're aware of his predilections."

Heat flooded Elizabeth's cheeks. She was *not* prepared to discuss Alexander's bedroom preferences with his mother. "Y-yes."

"Then you're aware of what that bracelet means."

Her hand moved to cover the cuff. God, this was not how she imagined this conversation. "He asked me if I'd wear it. As a symbol. A commitment without being a ring." Why couldn't she stop her mouth?

"Do I make you uncomfortable, Elizabeth?" Margaret's eyes sparkled, and she chuckled as Elizabeth shifted her gaze to the floor.

"That's an understatement."

"Would it help you to know that before Alexander's father and I decided to split, he wore my collar?"

The sip of champagne Elizabeth had taken to try to distract herself threatened to come out her nose, and she sputtered and coughed, finally wrapping the back of her hand over her mouth and nose. "You're…"

"A Mistress. I was. I suppose at my core, I still am. Though I have not *collared* a man in many years. I have a gentleman who keeps me company at my social engagements. He and I enjoy conversation, but alas, we are not compatible in the bedroom. But that's not what I wanted to discuss. What are your intentions towards Alexander?"

"I don't understand. I love him. He asked me to wear his cuff and I agreed."

Margaret offered her an indulgent smile. "You come from wealth, Elizabeth. Surely you must understand what I'm asking."

"I'm not after his money." She glared into Margaret's steely blue eyes. "I tried to have a document drawn up that stated that, but Ben refused to help me. Apparently, such a thing doesn't exist unless we're getting married. But if you want one, I'll give you my word right now." She bolted up, walked around Alexander's desk, and yanked open a drawer. There had to be a pad of paper somewhere. She found it in the second drawer she opened.

I, Elizabeth Bennett, declare on this day, the twenty-fifth of December, that should Alexander Fairhaven and I end our romantic relationship, that I will not accept a penny of his fortune. I further state that I will not, at any time, ask Alexander for any gift during the tenure of our relationship.

She signed the note and handed it to Margaret. "Is this good enough for you?"

Margaret barely glanced at the note before she tore it in half.

Elizabeth sputtered, "What did you do that for?"

"My sons are headstrong and independent, Elizabeth. Perhaps too much so. Alexander in particular. Nicholas may be older, but Alexander was always the more willful child. He assured me that your intentions were noble, and after speaking with you, I agree with him. This—" she waved a piece of the note, "—is admirable, but unnecessary. I have made my fortune being a proper judge of character and I believe yours to be strong and honest."

Elizabeth downed the remainder of her champagne and glanced over at the small wet bar in the corner of Alexander's office. Scotch might be a better choice for the rest of this conversation. "This was *so* not what I expected today."

"Honesty again. What *did* you expect?"

With a sigh, Elizabeth slumped back into the chair. "To be interrogated about my family."

"I know all about your family. Do you really think I wouldn't research my son's new love? You left a good job with your parents' company to come to Boston, where you worked hard for five years until this unpleasantness that nearly took my son's life. Both of your lives, in fact."

Though Margaret's tone was mild, almost kind, her words stung. "I never wanted Alexander involved. I tried…to keep him safe. But he wouldn't leave me alone, and if he hadn't…I would have died."

"Relax, dear. I'm trying to give you my blessing. Alexander looks at you the way I used to look at his father. We had twenty happy years together before the man decided he wanted to find another Mistress. He told me when he was dying that he regretted ending our marriage. I loved that man. But love is not always enough." A tinge of sadness colored Margaret's words, but she straightened her shoulders. "We have been away too long. I am rather shocked that Alexander hasn't interrupted us."

Elizabeth stood and offered Margaret her arm. The older Fairhaven accepted it and offered a feminine grunt as she rose. "Thank you. These old knees do not like getting up and down any longer. I don't recommend aging. Though I suppose it is better than the alternative."

The rest of the day passed with laughter, an exquisite spread for dinner, and figgy pudding for dessert. Margaret surprised everyone with a box of Christmas crackers that were opened around the hearth, accompanied by glasses of port. Darkness descended before the festivities wound down, and Elizabeth followed Kelsey into the kitchen for a glass of water close to midnight.

"You're getting rather cozy with Terrance," Elizabeth said, handing Kelsey a glass.

The petite redhead grinned and ran the tap. "He's cute."

"Kelse, he's…like Alexander. In the bedroom."

"Oh." Her smile faded. "I don't know if I can…I'm not like that." Her lower lip wobbled, and she rubbed her wrist.

Elizabeth reached for her friend's hands. "I didn't think I was either. But sweetie, I'm only telling you because I worry about you, and I didn't want him to spring that on you. I don't know him well enough to know if he'd be…understanding if you freaked out on him. I want to believe he would."

"He asked me out for coffee next week."

"Good." Elizabeth took a sip from her own glass and leaned against the gleaming black marble counter. Donatella and Samuel had cleaned up quickly after the lavish meal. "You should go and have a good time."

"He knows." Kelsey stared down at her feet. "He took my hand earlier. I saw the pity in his eyes when he touched my scar."

With a comforting hum, Elizabeth pulled Kelsey into a hug. "Maybe it wasn't pity. Maybe it was understanding. Give it a shot. It's only coffee. You haven't been on a date in a long time."

"You can say it. I haven't dated anyone since David died." Kelsey's words were muffled against Elizabeth's shoulder, and a little tremor ran down her spine. She pulled away. "I want to. He wouldn't want me to be alone for the rest of my life."

"No, he wouldn't. But take it slow. I know," she said, holding up her hand. "I'm the queen of mixed messages today. I want you to get out there and live again, sweetie. But I want you to be careful too."

"Is this a private party, or can any old gal butt in?" Toni strode into the kitchen on her stilettos, her short, brown curly hair bouncing along with her steps.

"I was asking Lizzie to explain this." Kelsey took Elizabeth's hand and held it up, letting the diamonds glint in the recessed lighting in the kitchen.

Toni joined them and ran her fingers over the bracelet. "Take it off, let's see it up close."

"I can't."

"What?" Both women frowned.

"It's locked. Kind of a sub thing," Elizabeth said, her cheeks flushing. "Unless I want to leave him, this stays on."

"Huh." Toni fingered the heart-shaped lock. "Well, you'd better hope you don't need an MRI or anything."

"You're not...upset?" Elizabeth's gaze traveled between her two best friends.

"He loves you. We've seen you together half a dozen times now, hon. And he took a bullet for you. Does he do anything you don't want him to do? Does he make you feel anything other than loved and respected?" Toni rested her hands on Elizabeth's shoulders and pinned her under an intense stare.

"No. Never."

"Then that's all we care about. This—" she slid her hand down to Elizabeth's wrist, "—isn't something I'd ever want. I don't understand why a man feels the need to *mark* a woman as his. Hell, I don't even want a ring when I get married. But that's me. If you're okay with this, and you swear to me that you always feel loved and respected, I'm good. But I'm going to ask you that question on a regular basis. We know what happened when Darren started taking over your life and we're *not* going to let that happen again. Okay?"

Elizabeth nodded, the tears burning at the corners of her eyes. "I love you, you know that? Both of you."

Kelsey wrapped both of them in her arms and rested her head against Elizabeth's. "We love you too. Now come on, I want another glass of port before the night's over."

8

$\mathcal{N}$ick trudged out of the bank on the twenty-sixth with a cashier's check tucked into his pocket. Ten thousand. Not nearly enough, but all he could scrape together over the past three days. After the first of the year, when a handful of his dividends paid out, he could manage another fifty thousand. Then after that, he'd sell his home, his car, and Candy's collar.

A wave of regret swamped him. He never should have asked her to wear the damn thing. She had a good heart, despite her complete lack of intelligence, and she'd trusted him. Three days before Christmas, he'd sat her down and told her he couldn't be her Dom anymore.

"Why not, sir?"

Nick took her hands, squeezing her fingers. "Because I'm damaged. I asked you to wear my collar because I didn't want to be alone. Not for any good reason. You're not happy, are you?"

His slave's pretty blue eyes shimmered. "I like it when you punish me, sir. When you're rough with me. But you don't do that much anymore."

With a shake of his head, Nicholas swore softly. "I can't punish you, Candy." If he tried, he'd lose control. Take his self-loathing out on the woman in front of him, and Candy wouldn't safeword. She didn't have the backbone. "I've got to let you go. I'll help you find a new Master. Make sure you're taken care of until you do. We can go to Chains together. I don't want you to end up with someone who treats you poorly."

Candy swept her hair off her neck and turned around so Nick could unlock her collar. "That's okay, sir," she said quietly.

When she faced him again, her delicate fingers brushed over her now unadorned neck. "I liked you, sir. And the parties. I hope you find someone new. You shouldn't be alone."

An hour later, he made his way through a back alley in the North End. Rapping three times on an unmarked door, he prayed the small pittance would be enough to hold them off until next week.

"I need to see Forlano," Nick said once the door opened.

"You'd better have his money," Mario, one of Forlano's enforcers spat as he let Nick pass. "I've got my girl's birthday tomorrow, and I don't want to have to beat the crap out of you and show up with busted knuckles."

With a shiver, Nick stared straight ahead as he headed down the long hall towards Forlano's office. "I'm working on it."

Damian Forlano sipped an espresso as he reclined at his desk. "Fairhaven. Given how many of my calls you've ignored this week, I didn't expect to see you here."

Nicholas carefully slid his hand into the inner pocket of his jacket. At his side, Mario tensed. "This is all I could get over the holiday."

As Forlano glanced at the check, he snorted. "This doesn't even cover your interest for the month. You've got some nerve showing your face here. Mario—"

"Wait! I can get you another fifty on the first, then the rest by the end of January." Nick backed away from Mario, but the massive enforcer hadn't left him an easy escape route.

"By the end of January," Forlano glanced down at his computer, tapped a few keys, and smiled, "you'll owe one-point-oh-nine million. I hope 'the rest' includes that extra ninety grand."

Nick blanched. "I…I'll get it. I—"

At Forlano's nod, Mario grabbed Nick's wrist, twisting hard enough that he felt something snap, and white, hot pain shot through him. His knees buckled, and he hit the ground. As he cradled his arm from his prone position, he forced himself to breathe.

Standing, Forlano peered down at him. "You'll pay off the remaining nine hundred thousand by New Year's Eve or I'll break something a lot more visible than your wrist. *Capisci?*"

Nick struggled to his feet. "I'll…get…your money," he wheezed, then turned and ran, praying he could still drive himself to Terrance's flat with only one good arm.

Two days later, Milos followed Elizabeth into the elevator at Fairhaven Tower. The tall bodyguard hadn't said a word to her beyond "Good morning, Miss Elizabeth," and she'd started to worry.

"Is everything all right?" She peered up at him as she turned her new office key over and over in her hand.

Milos flexed his fingers inside his new gloves. "I'm fine,

Miss Elizabeth. I didn't sleep well. That's all. Thank you for asking."

Something in Milos's dark brown eyes told her not to press. Not today. Soon, though.

Once they reached her floor, Elizabeth stepped out into a hallway with plush carpet and brightly lit walls lined with modern paintings full of bold colors and brash lines. They passed consulting firms, a law office, and two architectural firms before Elizabeth stopped at Suite 2506.

Sliding her key into the lock, Elizabeth held her breath. "Oh my God."

Three rooms greeted her, along with floor-to-ceiling windows overlooking the Charles River. The central reception area held only a cherry wood desk, phone, and chair. The office to the right was empty, but to the left, the larger private room held a bookcase, file cabinet, desk, and the nicest chair she'd ever seen.

Elizabeth trailed her hand over the polished wood of her desk with a smile. A furniture catalog on the corner of the desk bore a festive ribbon, along with a note.

Call my admin, Annabeth, to arrange delivery of any furnishings you need. Consider this a gift for making my brother happy.

—Nicholas

"They're never going to stop interfering, are they?" Elizabeth asked.

Milos chuckled. "No. Not likely." He backed up into the main office, pulling the door with him. "I'll be out here if you need me, miss."

As the door clicked shut, Elizabeth sank into her new chair, staring out the windows at the sparkling skyline. "I'm never going to get any work done with this view."

Despite her words, three hours later, she had a domain name, the beginnings of a website, and an email account. A legal pad held a long to-do list, item after item crossed out, still many more left undone.

In the short time she'd spent in her office, she'd reclaimed much of herself, and with a smile she couldn't dim if she tried, she packed up her laptop and notepad and then opened the outer door.

"Ready, miss?" Milos said, tucking a small tablet into the pocket of his black jacket.

"I'd like to go up to Nicholas's office and thank him for the offer of furniture. You can stay here—"

"Nice try," Milos said with a hint of a grin.

Elizabeth groaned. "As long as you're not going to follow me into the bathroom."

With an uncomfortable shift of his shoulders, Milos confirmed that yes, he probably would.

"Great. Come on. Let's go up then."

Milos glared at a group of three men who dared to get on the elevator with them. Elizabeth couldn't help her embarrassment. "Not everyone's out to hurt me," she said when they stepped out onto the executive floor.

"I'm just doing my job, miss."

Nicholas's office took up the entire floor. Elizabeth pressed the buzzer at the outer door, and a few moments later, a pretty raven-haired woman answered. "May I help you? Mr. Fairhaven isn't taking appointments today."

"Um, I'm Elizabeth Bennett, his brother's..."

The woman broke into a wide smile. "Oh, Elizabeth! I'm Annabeth. So good to meet you." She pumped Elizabeth's hand, then welcomed her into the suite. Annabeth had her own office that took up a third of the space, while Nicholas's glass-walled office filled the rest. Alexander's brother reclined in his chair, his back to her, staring out over the city.

"Did you need to order anything for your office?" Annabeth asked.

Something in Nicholas's posture worried Elizabeth, but she forced her gaze back to Annabeth. "No. I'm good for now. It's only me there."

"You'll need a sign for your door. I've already arranged to have a buzzer installed. Can I have the name of your firm?"

"Bennett Accounting."

Annabeth scrawled a note on a pad at her desk. "Gotcha." She rapped on one of the clear walls of Nicholas's office. As he turned, he forced a smile, then waved her inside.

When he stood, Elizabeth gasped. "What happened?" Nicholas's left wrist bore a stark white cast that peeked out from the unbuttoned cuff of his dress shirt.

"Stupid accident," he said quietly. "Slipped on some ice." By the uncomfortable set of his shoulders and the way his eyes shifted, Elizabeth didn't believe him, but she didn't know him well enough to press.

"Happy with your offices?" he asked as she sank into his guest chair.

"That view... How do you get any work done?" She sighed as the late afternoon light sparkled off the buildings. "The city's so beautiful."

Nicholas chuckled. "There are days... Somehow, I don't think you'll let it distract you for long, however. Alex thinks you'll rival CPH's former prestige within a year. I'm only sorry I can't offer you any work on the Fairhaven Exports accounts."

Holding up her hand, Elizabeth shook her head. "Don't be. Sorry, that is. There's no way I could work for you." She realized her gaffe as the words escaped, and flushed. "That came out wrong. I mean...it would be irresponsible for me to handle your accounts. You'd be the target of audits left and right because of my relationship with Alexander."

A grin tugged at Nicholas's lips and he arched a brow. "No wonder Alex loves you."

"You…that was a test," she said.

"Once or twice over this whole ordeal, I've wondered if Alex was so smitten he wasn't thinking clearly. Moving you in, risking his life for you, asking for a commitment so soon." He nodded towards her bracelet. "Before he took another step, I wanted to know what type of businesswoman you were."

"The n-next step? Oh God. Please tell me he's not going to propose on New Year's." She tried to still her fingers, failed, and shoved her hands under her thighs.

"Calm down, Elizabeth. As far as I know, Alex has no immediate plans to propose. But that bracelet is more of a commitment than he's ever made. And can you tell me that you'd turn him down?" Nicholas's intense blue-eyed gaze searched her face.

"I probably wouldn't turn him down," she admitted. "Even though it's too soon. I'd say yes, as long as he agreed to a very long engagement."

"That's what I thought."

Heavy fists pounded on the outer door. Nicholas tensed, then leapt up. "Stay here, Elizabeth." He sprinted out of his office. "Don't answer that and call security," he said to Annabeth.

Milos moved quickly towards Elizabeth, dark eyes scanning the room. He gestured towards Nicholas's private bathroom. "In there, miss. Don't come out until I say."

She rushed into the lavish washroom, but she didn't shut the door the entire way. Peering through the crack, she gasped as Nicholas admitted two large men. "Security is on their way, Mario. I'd suggest you get out now. I've still got two days to get Forlano his money."

Milos approached slowly, his hands flexing at his sides.

"Forlano doesn't trust you. Seems you showed up at the track last night."

Elizabeth covered her hand with her mouth. Oh God. He'd been gambling again.

"To settle my account, you piece of shite. To cash out so I could pay your boss. If he expects me to be able to hand over the money on the thirty-first, he damn well better leave me the fuck alone." Nicholas stood chest-to-chest with the man who'd spoken, and for a tense moment, Elizabeth feared they'd come to blows.

"How's the arm?" The man's lip curled into a smile, and he shoved Nicholas back. Alexander's brother stumbled, crashed into Milos, and winced as he righted himself. Annabeth whimpered from under her desk, and from Elizabeth's vantage point, she could see the young woman frantically typing on her phone.

Phone. Elizabeth fumbled for her purse, but the bag slid off her shoulder and landed on the floor with a loud thud. As she scrambled to gather her things, footsteps thudded towards her.

The door swung open. "Well, who is this?" A meaty hand grabbed her arm just as Milos reached the man.

Elizabeth stifled a grunt as strong fingers dug into her forearm, but Milos spun the man around, grabbed him by his leather jacket, and shoved him into the wall.

"If you know what's good for you, you will forget that you ever saw her. Do you know what sort of training the Greek Special Forces gives? I could kill you with a single blow. And then stuff you in the trash compactor piece-by-piece."

"Get the fuck out of my office," Nicholas growled as

Milos tossed the man who'd grabbed her into the main room. He struggled to his feet, cracked his neck, and balled his hands into fists.

Scrambling for her phone, Elizabeth was about to call 911 when three armed security guards burst through the outer office door. "What's going on here?" the tallest one asked.

"These gentlemen were just leaving," Nicholas replied. "See them out, will you?"

"Sir," Milos protested, but Nicholas shook his head and the bodyguard glared at him before returning to Elizabeth's side. "Get your things, miss. We're leaving. Now."

Elizabeth rushed to shove her sunglasses, gloves, and keys back into her purse. Once she'd retrieved her briefcase, she let Milos usher towards the outer door. Only one of the security guards remained, and he tried to stop them, but Nicholas intervened.

"This is Alexander's girlfriend. She wasn't a part of this. If you need to talk to her, call Alexander and he'll take care of it. Milos is her bodyguard. He'll be available by phone if you need anything."

"I will," Milos said. "But now we're leaving."

Milos took Elizabeth by the elbow and kept her close to his side. "If I tell you to run, at any time, drop whatever you're carrying and get somewhere public. Stop carrying your phone in your purse. On your person. Always. Do you understand?"

"Y-yes."

Elizabeth held it together until they were in the town car. Tucked in the back seat, she started to shiver. Milos cast a quick glance at her in the rearview mirror. "It will be warm in a few minutes, miss."

"I'm ok-kay." Her teeth chattered, and Milos flipped the switch on the heater, turning it up to maximum.

Tucking her head close to her knees, she tried to force calm breaths as Milos kept up a steady stream of anecdotes about his two nieces. By the time they arrived home, she'd stopped shivering, and her breathing had steadied. The sight of Alexander waiting for her drew a half-sob from her lips as the last of the tension melted away.

Alexander was pacing outside the house when Milos pulled up. He wrenched open the door and as soon as Elizabeth was in his arms, he finally steadied. "Nicholas called me. Shite, Elizabeth. Are you hurt?"

"N-no. Milos did his job." She melted against him, and Alexander wasn't sure he would ever let her out of his sight again.

Alexander led her inside with Milos on his tail. "I am going to throttle Nicholas. I already told him that I'm expecting him here within the hour and I want a full report from the building security detailing how those men made it past the front desk. Milos, take the rest of the night off. Elizabeth and I are staying in and William is sending over two additional men until I settle this with Nicholas's bookie."

"Yes, sir. Miss, good night."

"Milos, wait." Elizabeth grabbed the bodyguard's arm. "Thank you. I won't complain about you being my constant shadow again."

He offered her a small smile. "We'll see about that, miss. But you're welcome."

"Complaining?" Alexander tried to keep his tone light, but his anger rolled through him like a tidal wave, and he feared he'd soon be pulled under.

"He practically told me he was going to follow me into the bathroom."

Alexander paced. He'd overdone it today. Four miles on the treadmill while Elizabeth had been gone, two hours of conference calls, and then the stress of knowing Nicholas's indiscretions had put her in danger. But still he paced. Elizabeth had gone upstairs to take a bath, giving him some privacy to speak to Nicholas.

The door chimes, usually melodious and pleasant, augmented the headache throbbing behind his eyes. Samuel's low voice preceded Nicholas's rapid footsteps on the marble.

"Before you say anything," Nicholas said, "I know." His shoulders hunched as he joined Alexander in the parlor.

Alexander stalked over to the wet bar and poured himself a glass of scotch. He didn't offer Nicholas one. He wasn't inclined to give his brother anything at this point—other than nine hundred and fifty thousand dollars. "You put Elizabeth in danger."

"I'm paying my debts, Alex. I gave Forlano ten thousand dollars on three days ago, and still, he did this." Nicholas tugged on his sleeve, and Alexander noticed the cast for the first time.

"And you're surprised?" Alexander gestured towards the wet bar, even though all he wanted to do was throttle his brother. "You borrowed six hundred thousand from the man. How the hell did you get in so deep?"

Nicholas shook his head, then stared down at his feet. "Horses. Blackjack. A couple of overnight poker games. The interest is bloody robbery."

"Of course it is. *Organized crime*, Nicholas. How daft can you be?"

With no answer, Nicholas poured himself a glass of scotch, stared into the amber liquid, and sighed.

Finishing off his own drink, Alexander glared at his brother. "Call Forlano and arrange to meet him tomorrow. I'll send four men with you, along with a certified check for what you owe. As payment, you'll enter a twelve-step program. And if I ever catch wind of you gambling again, you're out as CEO of Fairhaven Exports."

"Alex."

"Shut it, Nicholas. I've had enough of your excuses. You have a gambling problem. Endangering Elizabeth and allowing men into your offices was the last straw. Mother always insisted that we deal with the consequences of our actions on our own, but your dalliances are affecting the woman I love, and I won't stand for that."

Nicholas rubbed the back of his neck. "I went to the track for the first time after I lost Lia. This past year…Candy and I weren't a good match. I tried, but…"

"Lia was an intelligent, beautiful woman." Alexander had only met Nicholas's former submissive a few times, but before Lia had been stricken with cancer, he'd thought Nicholas would marry her. "I'm sorry."

"I wanted someone in my life again, Alex. But I couldn't stand the idea of actually getting close to another woman. Candy didn't want a relationship. She wanted sex and punishment and parties. That sounded ideal. I've felt so empty, and gambling…filled the hole."

"Have you been to the track since she left?" Alexander sat across from Nicholas, unsure he'd ever be able to do so again comfortably.

"Yesterday." Nicholas held up his hand as Alexander's anger flared. "Just to cash out my account. I didn't place a bet, and I won't. I'll pay you back, Alex. I promise you."

"Yes. You will. You're my brother, and I love you. You helped me find my place in the world, and when Elizabeth needed us both, you helped protect her simply because I asked. But I can't trust you right now, and I don't know when that will change."

Nicholas nodded. Suddenly, he looked more like a chastised child than the man Alexander had looked up to for more than half of his life. With a quick flick of his wrist, Nicholas finished the scotch and then nodded.

"Thank you."

The two men rose, embraced, and walked to the foyer. "I'll find a Gamblers Anonymous meeting tomorrow as soon as I pay off Forlano," Nicholas said.

"See that you do."

"Please apologize to Elizabeth for me."

A twinge of pity tightened in Alexander's chest as Nicholas trudged through the door. "I will, brother. Good night."

9

_H_undreds of glittering lights in the crystal chandeliers sparkled, illuminating the Fairmont Hotel's Grand Ballroom. Poinsettias adorned every table, and boughs of holly and balsam were strung artfully over every window. Elizabeth let Alexander slide the silver wrap from her shoulders and hand it to a uniformed attendant at the coat check. She'd refused another loan of diamonds, suspecting that the citrine set from the Fire and Ice Ball were still in his closet somewhere, ready to be gifted at another occasion. Instead, she wore the rubies he'd given her for Christmas.

Her dress hugged every curve, a Vera Wang one-shoulder number in shimmery silver that had been tailored for her exact measurements. Silver heels had her almost at eye-level with Alexander. She'd already elicited the promise of a foot rub when the night was over. Of course, he'd extracted a promise of his own. One that had her hoping the tiny gray thong wouldn't let her down tonight. She'd be lucky if it didn't end up torn in two by the time they made it home.

"Are you warm enough, *chérie?*"

Alexander's voice sent heat sparking over her skin. He smelled like sandalwood, and as his lips brushed against her ear, goose flesh sprang up on her bare arms.

"I am now." More than a hundred partygoers spread out across the ballroom, drinking champagne out of crystal flutes and sampling hors d'oeuvres served by black-suited waiters wearing white gloves.

"Alexander, how are you?" An older gentleman in a white tux approached and held out his hand.

"Leonard, I'm well, thank you. May I introduce Elizabeth Bennett?"

"You are even lovelier in person, my dear. Leonard Blass, Treasurer for Fairhaven Business Group's Board of Directors."

Elizabeth shook his hand. "It's a pleasure."

"May I have a few moments alone with Alexander?"

"Elizabeth is my confidant in all things, she can stay." Alexander wrapped his arm around her waist, holding her close.

"This is...sensitive. The Board requires a few minutes of your time."

Though Alexander was about to protest again, Elizabeth patted his hand. "I'll get us some champagne and say hello to Ben." She brushed her lips against his ear. "Take your time."

Ben leaned against one of the bars set up in the corners of the room, and waved as she approached.

"Happy New Year," she said, nodding to the bartender when he offered her a glass of champagne.

"Elizabeth, you are a vision in silver." Ben took her hand and lifted it to his lips. "I'm surprised Alexander let you out of his sight with so many eligible bachelors here tonight."

"He's talking business." She wrinkled her nose and

swept her gaze across the room. Alexander was deep in conversation with Leonard off in a corner. The older man gestured as he spoke, obviously angry. When he poked Alexander in the chest, one of the security guards turned and started to approach, but Alexander waved him away, leaned down so he was face-to-face with Leonard, and glared as his lips moved slowly, probably giving the man an ultimatum or two. A few moments later, Alexander strode towards the bar, his shoulders stiff and his hands clenched into fists at his sides.

"Clearly that didn't go well," Ben muttered.

"Have you seen Nicholas?" Alexander asked.

Elizabeth took his hand and forced him to relax his fingers. "Are you okay?"

"The Board is threatening to oust Nicholas next week."

"Shit," Ben and Elizabeth replied in tandem.

"I need to make some calls. Unfortunately this cannot wait until after the party. I'm going to see if I can borrow of one of the hotel's conference rooms. Ben, I'll need you to join me." Alexander led the way towards the double doors, but stopped in his tracks a few feet away. "Shite."

"What is it?" Elizabeth hissed in his ear.

"Nicholas."

The elder Fairhaven headed towards them in a trim, black tuxedo that strained against his cast. Alexander made an almost feral sound. "I really did not want to deal with him tonight. Not after what happened the other day at his office."

"Let me." With a quick kiss to Alexander's cheek, Elizabeth extricated her hand from his death grip and made her way to Nicholas. Out of the corner of her eye, she saw Alexander and Ben head off Leonard and escort the man from the room.

"Happy New Year," Nicholas said, leaning in to kiss Elizabeth's cheek. "What's wrong? Why did Alex and Ben rush off?"

"Some charitable contribution that fell through. I'm glad you're here. Alexander is still paranoid about leaving me alone, and I really don't want to go sit in a conference room while he and Ben deal with that mess. Dance with me?"

"I'd love to." Nicholas offered Elizabeth his arm and she looked back in time to see Alexander mouth the words *thank you.*

They danced for half an hour, the holiday jazz tunes providing a mix of waltzes and more energetic dances. After the second song, Leonard left the ballroom with his phone pressed to his ear. Elizabeth tried to keep the conversation light, and Nicholas had her laughing with stories of Alexander as a child. They took a brief break for champagne, and were about to head back to the dance floor when Alexander returned to the ballroom. He looked tired, and his bow tie was askew.

"Come here," she whispered, tugging the errant silk until it lay flat and obedient once more. "That's better."

Nicholas and Ben wandered over to the bar, and Alexander wrapped his arms around Elizabeth. "Bloody hell. That was not how I wanted to spend the evening."

"What happened?"

"Nicholas will need to agree to a leave of absence for the first quarter of the year. If he does that and stays out of the papers, he'll be allowed to keep his position. Otherwise, I'll take over."

"Will he agree to it?" Elizabeth slid her hands underneath Alexander's tux jacket, feeling the hard muscles of his back. The tension he carried melted away as he nuzzled her neck, trailing kisses from her ear to the single strap of her dress.

"He will. They also agreed to let me be the one to tell him, which I will do tomorrow. We can relax the rest of the night."

"Good. Dance with me, Alexander."

"Gladly, *chérie*."

Elizabeth rested her head against the wood of the St. Andrew's Cross, her breath ragged and her desperate need to come gathering inside her like a storm. "Please," she begged. "I can't hold on."

The ache only intensified when Alexander pressed his naked body to hers. With two flicks of his hand, her wrists were freed, and she collapsed against him, which only gave him better access to her nipples.

As he carried her to the bed, she clutched at his shoulders, desperate to feel him buried deep inside her, to have him remove the blindfold so she could look into his eyes.

"You are a gift, Elizabeth," he said, drawing his thumb across her lips. "Are you mine, *chérie*?"

"Yes," she said, gasping as his fingers dipped inside of her and her back arched. "All yours."

"Then perhaps, I should unwrap you."

Nick Fairhaven needs some time to get his life in order. Alexander and Elizabeth have their happy-ever-after.

But what about hunky bodyguard, Milos?

Killing Elizabeth's attacker weighs on him, and he's convinced he'll never find happiness. Until he meets a Greek princess—literally—when she slips on the ice outside a local coffee shop.

New Year's Eve brings passion, but Elora hides pain Milos can never understand. Can they find a way to overcome their differences in time to toast at the stroke of midnight?

One-click ALL TIED UP FOR NEW YEAR'S now!

IF YOU LOVED CHRISTMAS SILKS, you'll love **BREAKING HIS CODE**, my sensual, geeky, and thrilling military romance.

She's a wounded warrior. He's a former SEAL and a hell of an online gamer. Can their love survive the transition to the real world?

After almost dying in an Afghanistan war zone, Cam found it easier to live in the virtual world than face reality. Until her flirtatious gaming buddy wants to meet face-to-face.

Even though West turns out to be a hunky former SEAL

who doesn't seem to mind her cane, her instincts still scream "RUN."

As she resolves to give love a shot, her career-making programming project comes under attack by a hacker. Does she have enough ammunition to fight on both battlefields?

West is haunted by the mission that took the lives of his team. So when he befriends a gamer and former Army ordnance specialist with scars of her own, their connection soothes something in his battered soul.

After the sharp-shooting beauty surpasses his wildest dreams, he's determined to break down the armored panels she's built around her heart. When his own worst fears return, he worries he won't be able to face the coming challenges alone.

With new enemies and old phantoms from their past closing in, can Cam and West find the courage to lower their defenses and heal their wounded hearts with love?

Breaking His Code is the first book in Away From the Keyboard series of explosive military romantic suspense novels. If you like diehard female veterans, sexy cyber romance, and emotional journeys of healing, then you'll love this heartfelt tale of love after war.

One-click **BREAKING HIS CODE** now!

You can also join my Facebook group, **Patricia's Unstoppable Forces**, for exclusive giveaways, sneak peeks of future books, and the chance to see your name in a future novel!

P.S. Reviews are like candy for authors.

Did you know that reviews are like chocolate (or cookies or cake) for authors?

They're also the most powerful tool I have to sell more books. I can't take out full page ads in the newspaper or put ads on the side of buses.

Not yet, anyway.

But I have something more powerful and effective than ads.

A loyal (and smart) bunch of readers.

Honest reviews of my books help bring them to the attention of other readers.

If you've enjoyed this book, I'd be eternally grateful if you could spend just five minutes leaving a review (it can be as short as you like) on the book's Amazon page.

Turn the page for an excerpt from **ALL TIED UP FOR NEW YEAR'S**.

SNEAK PEEK - ALL TIED UP FOR NEW YEAR'S

Elora

*P*ackages scatter along the icy walk, tumbling from my grasp as I scramble to stop the inevitable. But as my ass hits the cement and the air leaves my lungs in a violent hiccup, tears burn the corners of my eyes. I should know better. I do know better. Winter in Boston can be dangerous when you can only see out of one eye and your depth perception sucks. Add in a snowplow that kicks up frigid icicles and decides to hurtle them towards you at light speed on a brilliantly sunny day after a snowstorm, and boom! Disaster.

"Oh my God, are you all right?" A woman rushes over, golden hair swinging free, a long, leather coat brushing her knees. She kneels in the slush, resting a gloved hand on my shoulder. "Say something."

"F-fine," I offer once my breath returns. I feel more

stupid than injured, though the man she's with extends a hand to help me up, and I wince as I try to get my feet under me. He immediately sidesteps me, and his strong hands cup my elbows as he sets me to rights again. "Thank you."

Now that I'm eye level with my rescuer, I recognize her. "How many of those boxes did you have?" Elizabeth Bennett, soon-to-be-wife of Boston's richest man, frowns as the wall of muscle with her retrieves my boxes.

"Fifteen." I try to help, but my boot catches another patch of ice, and I skid into Elizabeth, sending us both careening into a parked car. "Son of a motherless goat!"

"Go inside," the man—who is definitely not her fiancé, bodyguard maybe?—says. "I'll retrieve your things." His accent reminds me of home, and as he picks up the next box, his dark gaze seeks me out. Elizabeth takes my arm, but I can't move. Even through his thick wool coat, I can tell he's massive. Six-foot-four if he's an inch, at least two hundred pounds, with cheekbones from the gods and a square jaw dusted with stubble.

Elizabeth clears her throat. "Can you walk?"

"Usually. Today, the jury's still out." I let her help me into Artist's Grind, my favorite coffee shop and one of the places I sell the rings, necklaces, and earrings I make, and Elizabeth settles me at one of the small bistro tables in the center of the small space. Devan, the owner, talks with a customer, and her partner, a sweet, yet gruff man named Mac, hauls a weighty bag of coffee in from the back room.

"What do you want? The coffee's on me." She holds out her hand. "I'm Elizabeth Bennett."

"I know." I wince, shake my head, and grip her fingers firmly. "I'm sorry. Elora Kalivas. I swear, my manners—and my balance—are usually better."

"I've lived in Boston for seven years, and I still take at

least one tumble every winter. What are you drinking?" She turns toward Devan and waves.

I should protest. After all, I ran into her. But the fine Greek specimen—and I mean that literally: if he's not from Greece, I'll eat my own winter coat—pulls open the door, stamps his feet to clear them of snow, and catches my eye. I can barely mumble, "Pour-over...whatever Devan recommends," before my mouth goes dry and my palms dampen inside my gloves.

Despite the problems with my right eye, the left works just fine, thank you very much, and I can't help but gawk as he sets my boxes down on the table in front of me, each one intact, albeit damp from the snow. "You need better boots."

"What?" I barely register his words, so taken with his olive skin and dark eyes. And the accent. Let's not ignore that, shall we? "Oh. Boots." I look down, and my cheeks catch fire. At least my complexion assures me I don't look as embarrassed as I feel. "I have some. I just...they're getting resoled, and this storm came out of nowhere." The boots aren't the problem. My traitorous body is. But he can't know that. I don't look disabled. The fact that the whole right side of my body is weak isn't evident by looking at me. Hell, even my blind eye doesn't look much different. My iris is a little paler on that side, a little cloudy, but most people never notice. Or they stare, thinking that there's something off with me, but not knowing what.

He frowns, his trim brows drawn together, making a furrow I want to smooth away. "I know you."

"No, I don't think so." I'd definitely remember meeting him before. Though if he's Greek... But seventeen years is a long time. Not to mention two surgeries, twelve inches less hair, and twenty extra pounds. Okay, twenty-five.

"Milos Sagona." He offers his hand, but before I respond,

Elizabeth joins us, balancing three cups of coffee in her hands. Milos accepts one with a nod and sits at the next table, between Elizabeth and the front door. His gaze never stills, flitting from patron to patron, the door, and Devan and Mac. I'm spared further abject staring by the cup of coffee and smiling woman next to me. "There, that's better," she says. "Where were you headed all loaded down like that?"

"Here, actually." I motion to Devan and start to rise, but my right leg protests the effort. I guess I did a little more damage than I thought. As I lower myself back down, Devan rushes over and greets me with a hug and a kiss on the cheek. I hold onto her a little longer than usual, still kicking myself for ruining the gorgeous Christmas wrapping job on at least half of my wares. When I finally pull away, Devan's smiling, and I can't help responding in kind. "The boxes got a little wet. But I'll bring some fresh ones down this afternoon once the ice melts a little."

"Oh hon, don't worry about that. I'll send Mac to walk you home, and he can cart them back, okay?"

I try not to show how much her offer means to me. I do okay most of the time. The headaches don't bother me more than once or twice a week, and I haven't had a seizure in a month. But a brief halo flashes behind Devan's brown curls, and I know I need to be careful today. "Thanks. Do you want me to arrange the display?" My voice drops to a whisper, and I hope she hears the plea behind my words.

"God, no. That's what you pay me the big bucks for."

I snort as she pats my back and then practically dances off to the rear of the shop. Artist's Grind is half coffee shop, half local artist mecca. When I moved into my walk-up two years ago, I discovered Devan—and the shop—after I unpacked my broken coffee pot. Never pay college kids to pack your breakables and offer them beer before the packing's done. Not my finest hour. With our shared love of coffee and Devan's outgoing personality, I found myself spending more and more time here until we'd crossed the line from business associates to friends.

Devan stands back and peruses the shelves bearing all manner of artisan crafts and gifts: scarves, mittens, stained glass art, hand-stamped stationery, Mac's metal work, and my jewelry. Today's delivery included six rings, a dozen pendants, five sets of earrings, and three bracelets. I work in silver, primarily, though I've branched out into gold of late, when I can afford the materials. With a practiced eye, Devan maneuvers some of the display racks. "Are prices in the boxes?"

I nod and turn my focus to my coffee. "Thank you, Elizabeth. Caffeine is the only thing capable of saving my morning." I let my hair fall over my right eye and peer over my cup at the wealthy—and soon-to-be wealthier—woman cupping a mug like it contains the nectar of Heaven. I've seen her in the papers, of course, but in person, she's lovelier. Fresher. Real. Of course, the rock of Gibraltar on her ring finger chases a bit of that realism away, but tiny lines tighten around her lips, and her eyes are bloodshot. Up close, she looks like she needs a week at a spa. Or at least a good night's sleep. "You come here often?"

"Every chance I get. Though lately, I've been too busy. I finally told my fiancé I needed a day off from wedding planning. I swear the man has minions. Why can't they take over for a while?"

"Minions?" I can't help but laugh. "What did he say?" The idea that this woman speaks to Alexander Fairhaven— eats with Alexander Fairhaven, has sex with Alexander Fairhaven even—fills me with wonder. He's not my type—or at least, I don't think he is. The closest I've gotten to the man is knowing Devan and Mac. Earlier this year, Mac designed a sculpture for the lobby of the new Fairhaven Tower. A few stories were shared over a six-pack of beers one long, summer night. Stories I'll never repeat. Mac walked in on an office tryst in the middle of the installation. Even now, I fight my blush at the thought.

Elizabeth sips her drink and leans back in her chair. "He offered to plan the whole damn thing himself. But that's even worse. The last time I told him to make a decision so I didn't have to, he called Vera Wang to design my dress. I could have fed a third-world country for the cost of that dress. I said no. Found the perfect dress at a second-hand shop on Houston Street. A few hours of alterations, and no one's ever going to know I didn't have it designed just for me." She beams with pride and twirls a diamond bracelet around her wrist. A platinum lock secures the cuff, and I can't help but wonder if the rumors are true.

"The wedding's in less than a month, isn't it?" I thought I read something about a New Year's Eve ceremony and a grand ball. "What can you possibly have left to do?"

"Only the most important thing ever." Elizabeth sighs and stares down at her hands. "I hate every wedding ring design the jeweler's come up with. They're all 'befitting a man of Alexander's station—and the woman he marries.' But they don't fit me."

"What do you want, then?" I speak the language, and I have a fair idea what a "man of Alexander's station" should want. I don't blame Elizabeth a bit for rejecting those designs. No personality. No heart.

A small smile graces her lips. "I want my grandmother's wedding ring. It's long gone now, or at least out of my reach, but…" She looks down at my hands and gasps. "Oh my God.

Where did you get this?" She takes my left hand and runs her index finger over the ring I wear on my thumb. The design resembles the gears on the Doctor's cradle from "A Good Man Goes to War," with a pale green peridot in the center. One of my first designs—I haven't removed the ring in ten years, other than for cleaning and my last surgery.

"It's mine. My design, I mean."

Elizabeth springs up and heads for Devan. "Why didn't you tell me you knew someone who designed jewelry?" She peers into the open boxes spread out on the display tables.

"I didn't know you needed someone. Elora's fantastic. I can't keep her earrings in stock." Devan slips away to take care of a new customer as Elizabeth makes all sorts of oohs and ahs over my designs. The attention is flattering. I love what I do, but though I know I have talent, the idea that I can compete with the hunk of ice on her hand never occurred to me.

"How quickly could you design me a ring? Or two?" She hasn't left the display tables, so I rise and limp over to join her, my hip still tender. "These three are so close. I love the —" she gestures with her hands.

"Whorls."

"Yes, and the filigree. The inset there. And on that one, the etching is gorgeous. Marry," she chuckles, "all three of those designs, and maybe a little bit of yours. Can you do that in three weeks?"

Design a ring for a billionaire's wedding? The thought terrifies me, but Elizabeth's enthusiasm is infectious, and as she clutches my hand and pleads with me, I can't help but agree. "I have a sketchbook in my bag. Let me rough out a couple of ideas for you now. Do you have a few minutes?"

"Absolutely. Let me call Alexander and tell him to cancel his meeting with Neil Lane. Thank God." She throws her arms around me and squeezes. "You're saving my wedding. Truly."

I highly doubt that, but still, I hug her back. After all, she did prevent my ass from freezing to the sidewalk. As I reach the table with our coffees and then withdraw my weathered sketchbook, Milos approaches with a smartphone in his hand. "Elora Kalivas. I remember seeing you on television when I was young. The state dinner." His brows furrow, and he angles his head. "But after that, you disappeared. The papers spoke of rumors. The *vrykolakas* from Santorini. What really happened? Why did you leave Greece?"

Oh God. He knows. A flare of light draws my attention, but as soon as I turn my head, the brightness disappears.

"Shit," I whisper as my messed-up brain decides now's the time to hit me with one of the cluster headaches that always precede a seizure. I've got ten minutes, maybe fifteen, before my body betrays me. Milos steadies me when I sway, and he tries to brush the hair away from the right side of my face.

"Are you all right, Elora?"

He says my name with such reverence, I fear his voice will drown me. I can't do this. I need my pills, my cat, and my bed. Wrenching my arm free, I tug my bag over my head. "Elizabeth, I'm sorry. I have to go. Now. My number's on the cards there. Call me tomorrow." With a last look into Milos's dark eyes, I flee, praying I'll reach my apartment without another fall.

Milos

Elizabeth stares after Elora, confusion pinching her brows. "Milos?"

I stare down at my boots and at the drops of melted snow that gather around the chair Elora just occupied. "I am sorry, Miss Elizabeth. I spoke out of turn."

She arches a brow. "Sit. I think you need to tell me a little bit about Elora Kalivas. And how you know her."

Embarrassment warms my neck as I fold my body into the small cafe chair across from Elizabeth. Elora's card draws my gaze, and I run my fingers over the embossed lettering. "Years ago, back in Greece, the national papers claimed she was a vampire."

Elizabeth's eyes dance with her laughter, though she must see the sorrow written on my face, for she quickly stops. "A vampire. And people believed this?"

"Many of the small towns in my country…the old stories linger. Children stolen in the night, blood painted on the doors. If pressed, most would admit there is no such thing as a *vrykolakas*, but a politician's daughter—well, it is much like in America. Those in the spotlight have targets on their backs."

"What happened to her?" She leans forward and rests her elbows on the table.

"I don't know the details. I was only seventeen when she disappeared from the public eye, and I enlisted in the military a month or two later. She made some sort of scene at a state dinner, and then her father lost the election. No one ever saw her in public after that." I shake my head. "Why did I remind her of that public shame?"

Though my words were meant more for myself than Elizabeth, she lays her hand on my arm. "Boot-in-mouth disease?

Brought on by a sudden attraction to a beautiful woman?"
Her understanding smile only serves to heighten my shame,
and I pull away to stare into my coffee. "Milos, I'd have to be
deaf not to hear how your voice changed when you spoke to
her." She nudges the card towards me. "Call her. Apologize.
Ask her out."

"I can't. She deserves better."

"Better?" Elizabeth snorts. "You saved my life. Alexander's life. You love your family, I've seen you stop the limo to
let a family of ducks cross the road, and I'm pretty sure the
last time I forced you to take a day off, you spent it volunteering down at the food bank. I'm not sure how much better
of a man you could possibly be. Call. Her."

After more than a year of working for Alexander
Fairhaven and protecting his fiancé, I've learned the futility
of arguing with Elizabeth. I take the card once she's copied
the number for herself, and as my hand dips into my pocket, I
catch a whiff of Elora's perfume.

I could be a much better man. Greece's princess deserves
more than a killer. Even if my crime did save two other lives.
I'll call her, because Elizabeth will hound me if I don't. But
once I apologize, I'll walk away.

Flipping my coat collar up against the stinging snow, I
turn towards my apartment. Once Elizabeth's bosses had
been sentenced, I'd no longer had to live in the staff's quarters. Despite the proximity to the ritzy neighborhood my
employer lives in, this place is affordable. Though I've often
wondered if Mr. Fairhaven had something to do with that.

Nights like this always remind me of the shooting. Elizabeth's scream. Mr. Fairhaven's blood staining the dingy snow. Carl's sightless eyes staring up at me. Years in the Greek military prepared me to fight. They did not prepare me to kill. Or rather, to forgive myself for killing. I had no choice. The assassin would have killed Elizabeth. Mr. Fairhaven spent days in the hospital and weeks recovering at home. Yet, even a year later, I still wake with the scent of gunpowder in my nose.

A letter from my mother waits in my mailbox. Even after I bought her a computer—and my sister taught her how to use email—she still writes to me. I tear open the card as my frozen burrito cooks in the microwave.

Dear Milos,

I hope you are well. Your father and grandmother send their love and hope you will be able to come home sometime next year. The vineyards are beautiful now that we have rented them to Mr. and Mrs. Elkenos. The profits are not high, but at least your father does not need to walk the hills every day.

Alesia and Doriana have talked of nothing but the big Christmas tree at Boston Commons and the ice skating. Will you be able to take us there when we visit?

Is there anyone special in your life? I worry about you, my son. More so around the holidays. What you went through last year...no one should have to carry that burden. You should be surrounded by love, not living alone, microwaving your food, with only television for company.

Please take care of yourself, Milos. The next few weeks will pass very slowly for me. Slower still because Dori asks me when we need to leave for the airport every few hours.

Love,

Mama

The microwave beeps, and I chuckle at Mama's telepathy. She has never been one to believe in the spiritual, but she's never missed the mark in any of her letters, despite my best efforts to only let her see the good in my life.

As I sink down onto the couch with my burrito and a beer, something sharp pokes my leg through my black pants. Elora's card. Running my finger over the embossed lettering, I wonder why Greece's fragile princess is hiding in the States. And how I can convince her to have coffee with me.

Buy All Tied Up For New Year's now!

ALSO BY PATRICIA D. EDDY

Away From Keyboard

Dive into a steamy mix of geekery and military might with the men and women of Emerald City Security and North-West Protective Services.

Breaking His Code

In Her Sights

On His Six

Second Sight

By Lethal Force

Fighting For Valor

Call Sign: Redemption

Midnight Coven

These novellas will take you into the darker side of the paranormal with vampires, witches, and more.

Forever Kept

Immortal Hunter

Elemental Shifter

Hot werewolves and strong, powerful elementals. What's not to love?

A Shift in the Water

A Shift in the Air

By the Fates

Check out the By the Fates series if you love dark and steamy tales of witches, devils, and an epic battle between good and evil.

By the Fates, Freed

Destined: A By the Fates Story

By the Fates, Fought

By the Fates, Fulfilled

In Blood

If you love hot Italian vampires and and a human who can hold her own against beings far stronger, then the In Blood series is for you.

Secrets in Blood

Revelations in Blood

Holidays and Heroes

Beauty isn't only skin deep and not all scars heal. Come swoon over sexy vets and the men and women who love them.

Mistletoe and Mochas

Love and Libations

Restrained

Do you like to be tied up? Or read about characters who do? Enjoy a fresh BDSM series that will leave you begging for more.

In His Silks

Christmas Silks

All Tied Up For New Year's

In His Collar

ABOUT THE AUTHOR

I've always made up stories. Sometimes I even acted them out. I probably shouldn't admit that my childhood best friend and I used to run around the backyard pretending to fly in our Invisible Jet and rescue Steve Trevor. Oops.

Now that I'm too old to spin around in circles with felt magic bracelets on my wrists, I put "pen to paper" instead. Figuratively, at least. Fingers to keyboard is more accurate.

Outside of my writing, I'm a professional editor, a software geek, a singer (in the shower only), and a runner. I love red wine, scotch (neat, please), and cider. Seattle is my home, and I share an old house with my husband and cats.

I'm on my fourth—fifth?—rewatching of the modern *Doctor Who*, and I think one particular quote from that show sums up my entire life.

"We're all stories, in the end. Make it a good one, eh?" — *The Eleventh Doctor, Doctor Who*

I hope your story is brilliant.

You can reach me all over the web…
patriciadeddy.com
patricia@patriciadeddy.com

Made in the USA
Coppell, TX
02 June 2022

78411144R00066